He couldn't fail this kid.

She didn't deserve that after all she'd been through. But Mason was probably the last person in the world who should be trusted with responsibility for her.

A cold hand seemed to squeeze his heart. What did he know about being a father? His own father hadn't set much of an example.

He glanced at his watch. He was about to meet the daughter he'd never known existed—for the first time. And his life would change irrevocably. But it already had, hadn't it? It had started to change months ago, at the class reunion. He just hadn't recognized it at the time.

* * *

REUNION REVELATIONS: Secrets surface when old friends—and foes—get together.

MARTA PERRY

has written everything from Sunday school curriculum to travel articles to magazine stories in twenty years of writing, but she feels she's found her home in the stories she writes for the Love Inspired line. Marta lives in rural Pennsylvania, but she and her husband spend part of each year at their second home in South Carolina. When she's not writing, she's probably visiting her children and her five beautiful grandchildren, traveling or relaxing with a good book. Marta loves hearing from readers, and she'll write back with a signed bookplate or bookmark. Write to her c/o Steeple Hill Books, 233 Broadway, Suite 1001, New York, NY 10279, e-mail her at marta@martaperry.com or visit her on the Web at www.martaperry.com.

Final Justice

MARTA PERRY

Steeple
Hill®

Published by Steeple Hill Books™

Special thanks and acknowledgment to
Marta Perry for her contribution to the
REUNION REVELATIONS miniseries.

STEEPLE HILL BOOKS

Steeple
Hill®

ISBN-13: 978-0-373-44294-2
ISBN-10:   0-373-44294-7

FINAL JUSTICE

Copyright © 2008 by Harlequin Books S.A.

www.SteepleHill.com

Printed in U.S.A.

If you search for good, you will find favor,
but if you search for evil, it will find you.
—*Proverbs* 11:27

This story is dedicated to my own dear college friends, including Cynthia, Liz, Ginny, Phyllis, Babs, Barbara and any others whose names I've missed. And, as always, to Brian, with much love.

PROLOGUE

He was about to meet the daughter he'd never known existed. He sat alone on a park bench, watching the spring sunshine filter through veils of Spanish moss and trying to make sense of the changes that had turned his life upside down.

Across the park, a father pushed his child on the rustic swing set. The little girl—four or five, maybe—laughed, her light voice floating toward him on the sultry air.

"Higher, Daddy. Higher."

A cold hand seemed to squeeze his heart. What did he know about being a father? His own father certainly hadn't set much of an example. In fact, if his father were alive today, he'd be quick to point out that this was just another opportunity for him to fail someone.

He couldn't fail this child. She didn't deserve that after all she'd been through. But he was probably the last person in the world who should be trusted with the responsibility for her.

He glanced at his watch. They'd come soon, and his life would change irrevocably.

But it already had, hadn't it? It had started to change months ago. He just hadn't recognized it at the time.

ONE

Magnolia College's ten-year reunion was in full swing on a warm southern evening. Jennifer Pappas stood alone near the French doors that opened to the terrace, wondering what on earth had made her agree to come.

The Mossy Oak Inn on the edge of the college campus prided itself on elegant service, and the staff had outdone itself tonight. Discreet waiters circulated with trays of hors d'oeuvres, while a string combo played a delicate counterpoint to the reliving of college memories. The scent of roses mingled with that of expensive perfume, almost dizzying in its impact.

She took an automatic step back from the exuberant greetings going on between two women who'd just, apparently, found each other after ten years and were determined to catch up on everything that had happened since.

That was what she feared the most tonight—that seemingly innocuous question: What have you been doing since graduation?

How do I answer that, Father? She sought refuge in prayer, as she always did, focusing inward and shutting out the clamor of insistent voices rising above the chamber music. *How could I talk about the day-care center I ran in Syracuse without mentioning how it ended?*

A shudder touched her heart, and she steeled herself against the memories, locking them away. She wouldn't dwell on the past. She'd started a new life. That was what this was all about, wasn't it?

But she'd been back in Magnolia Falls for over a month now, and she still hadn't found her balance. She was beginning to wonder if she ever would.

Her gaze fell upon Steff Kessler, a fellow class member who was now the alumni director for Magnolia College. Steff had seemed eager to renew their college friendship, but even with Steff, she'd held back. How did you explain to anyone, let alone a friend, what it was like being arrested, charged, fingerprinted?

No one here knew the truth except for Pastor Rogers and her father. Dad kept insisting her life would be easier once she'd confided in a few friends, but she couldn't do that. She couldn't bear the possibility that they'd look at her with contempt.

The French door moved behind her, and someone stepped through. She turned, startled, and found herself face-to-face with Mason Grant.

"Mason." Her heart twisted. Once she'd considered Mason one of her closest friends. Then, quite suddenly in the middle of their senior year, he'd shut her out, along with everyone else he'd been close to.

According to Steff, that was still the case. Steff hadn't expected him to show up tonight, even though he still lived in Magnolia Falls.

"Jennifer Pappas." He looked as startled as she felt. "I haven't seen you since—well, since graduation."

"Ten years." She managed a smile. "How many times do you suppose those words have been said tonight?"

That brought an answering smile to his face. "Too many, I suppose. And they're still at it." He glanced at the noisy crowd, seeming to search for familiar faces, giving her a moment to take a quick look at him.

Her first thought was that he hadn't changed. Tall, lean, he still had the sinewy build of a basketball player, evident even in the perfectly tailored tux he wore. He had regular features, dark blond hair that was always a little tousled despite his best efforts, hazel eyes—

And there she saw the difference.

Guarded. Once they'd been dancing eyes, but now they hid secrets. Maybe others would be fooled by the cheerful facade, but she recognized the expression. It was one she saw daily in her mirror.

What is it, Mason? What's changed you? What's put those lines around your eyes and given that wary set to your mouth?

That was not a question she could ask, since it was one she wouldn't answer herself.

He brought his attention back to her, his lips easing in a smile. "Actually, I heard that you were back in town."

"Probably at church." Mason's family had been long-time members of Magnolia Christian Church, although she hadn't seen him at services there since she'd been back. "Pastor Rogers has hired me to run the church nursery school. I'll also be doing the after-school program starting in September."

His gaze evaded hers. "I must have heard somewhere else. I haven't been at church lately. The stores keep me too busy for much of anything but work."

That would be the chain of sporting-goods stores Mason had inherited when his father died during their senior year. Anyone might use that as an excuse. But Mason looked lost and alone somehow, just for an instant, before he veiled the emotion with a bland, cool mask.

Jennifer's heart twisted. She wanted to reach out to him, to soothe the hurt she sensed in him just as she'd automatically run to comfort a crying child.

"Too busy for your faith? For your friends? What happened, Mason?" The words were out before she could censor them.

He looked startled, as well he might. "What do you mean? Nothing's happened."

She touched his sleeve, feeling hard muscle tense at her touch beneath the fine fabric of his tux, knowing it was a mistake to push but unable to resist her engrained need to help.

"We were good friends, before you walked away from all of us. Why did you do that?" She still remembered the pain, even though it had been ten years—the grief she felt at losing her friend and not knowing why.

Mason's smile seemed frozen on his face. "Things happened, senior year, things none of us could control. Maybe you've forgotten I was the college pariah after losing the championship game for the team."

She made a small sound of distress. "None of your friends blamed you for that, and anyone who did was an idiot. We wanted to help you then, but you shut us out. Can't you let us make up for it now?"

"There's no changing what's done." He jerked a nod toward the chattering crowd. "You think any of them would really go back, even if they could? No matter how many fond memories they dredge up tonight, at some level they all know the reality. It's far better for all of us to leave the past alone."

She was too shocked by the bitterness in his voice to respond. Maybe he read that in her face, because for a moment she saw the old Mason.

He clasped her hand in his, squeezing it gently. "Your heart always was too tender for your own good, Jennifer. But I'm glad you're back, all the same." He let her hand go slowly, almost reluctantly. "We both ought to circulate. I'm sure plenty of old friends are eager to greet you."

And then he turned and slipped away into the crowd.

TWO

"I'm telling you the truth. We found Penny Brighton Kessler. She admitted she killed Josie, and the picture she had of the child she claims is her daughter looked exactly like Josie Skerritt."

Mason stared at Kate Brooks across the red-and-white checked tablecloth at Burt's Pizzeria, the food turning to ashes in his mouth. This couldn't be happening. It couldn't.

In the months since the reunion, he'd broken his habit of isolation to meet with a few old classmates occasionally—Kate, Parker Buchanan, Steff Kessler and Trevor Whittaker. And Jennifer Pappas, of course, always Jennifer.

Despite their rocky beginning at the reunion, despite the fact that Jennifer's desire to reach out to him threatened the secrets that burdened him, he couldn't seem to stay away from her. It was friendship, he told himself. That was all he felt.

And he'd needed friendship, as long-hidden secrets began to emerge over the past few months. First came the discovery of the body, hidden near the library, when Trevor's construction company broke ground for the new library wing. Initially, he hadn't imagined that had anything to do with his class, his friends.

But gradually the circle tightened. The body had been there since the December after their graduation, making a tenuous link to his class. People had been drawn into the mystery, trying to locate any missing class members.

Then the body had been identified as that of Josie Skerritt, one of their close circle of friends from Campus Christian Fellowship. No one could remember having seen her since graduation. His nightmares had started then. It had grown worse with the revelation that Josie had had a baby.

Everyone from their small group of college friends had been questioned. Everyone had, he supposed, been suspected in some way. Each time they were together, no matter how they tried to ignore it, the conversation would go back to Josie. How did she die? Why? What happened to the child she'd apparently had not long before her death?

Jennifer moved slightly, her hands seeming to push something away. Her velvety brown eyes were troubled. "I don't understand. Are you saying that Penny stole Josie's child?"

The words echoed in his mind, mocking him, reminding him. Josie's child. Josie had a child. If Kate's suspicions were right, a daughter.

Whose child? His stomach churned. *Not mine. It couldn't be mine.*

Parker Buchanan, sitting next to Kate at the round table, put his hand over hers in a possessive movement. "You do remember that the police told us to keep quiet about this, don't you?"

Kate wrinkled her nose at him. "Listen, Jennifer's the one who figured out where Penny was. The police know she has to be warned about Penny. Anyway, she's one of my best friends."

A faint flush touched Jennifer's smooth olive skin, as if it pleased her to be called that. She looked cool and put together, even in jeans and a simple knit shirt, but he knew that outward appearance masked a sensitive spirit.

"We shouldn't ask," she said to Kate. "But if you want to tell us—"

Kate leaned forward, pushing aside the remains of her mushroom pizza. The eager sparkle in her eyes said she was about to be indiscreet.

"Penny admitted she was trying to frame Parker for Josie's murder." Indignation filled Kate's voice. "She's off her rocker if you ask me. She showed me the photograph, and when I said the little girl looked like Josie, she flew into a rage. She was going to kill me and frame Parker." She touched the sling in which her arm rested. "If Parker hadn't gotten there in time, she'd have succeeded."

"I'm a real hero, I am." Parker, as always, was faintly self-mocking. "I let her get away."

"You were taking care of me." Kate gave him a look that would have shown a blind man how she felt about him.

Well, good for them. They both deserved a little happiness. Unlike him.

He shook his head, trying to get a grip on the situation. "Did Penny admit the child was Josie's?" Even articulating the words shook him.

"Not exactly." Kate frowned. "But honestly, if you'd seen the photo, you couldn't help but notice. Same heart-shaped face, same brown hair and brown eyes—"

"Lots of people have brown hair and brown eyes." Steff Kessler's voice was sharp, a reminder to everyone that Penny had been married briefly to her brother, Adam.

"Same wistful expression," Kate finished. "You know how Josie would look sometimes. Like a little girl lost. That's how this child looks."

That shook him. He remembered that look all too well.

"Penny claimed her daughter was Adam's child." Steff's voice tightened. Though it had been ten years, she still felt the loss of her brother, dead in an apparent boating accident soon after his elopement with Penny. "But she wouldn't agree to a DNA test, and my parents never believed it."

"You see?" Kate's voice was triumphant. "She could hardly agree to a DNA test on the child if the baby was really Josie's."

"That poor child." Jennifer's thoughts went straight to the child, of course. "If this is true, I can't imagine what it must be like for her. Where is she? Not with Penny, I hope."

"In a private boarding school in Charleston," Parker said. "I managed to hear one of the police officers say that, but then they clammed up. Anyway, officially the cops are after Penny for the attack on Kate, but I imagine they're looking hard at her for Josie's death."

Penny, suspected of murder. She'd been wild enough,

bragging about having been kicked out of more schools than she could count, driving her elderly Charleston parents to declare Magnolia College her last chance. But murder—

It seemed impossible, but hardly less so than any of the other things that had rocked Magnolia Falls and the college since the body was discovered.

Mason's cell phone vibrated. He was tempted to ignore it, but he didn't do that, ever. It could be some crisis at one of the branch stores. Worse, it could be his mother's assisted-living facility.

He checked the number, found it was one he didn't recognize and answered, turning slightly away from the table.

"Mason Grant." He kept his voice low.

For a moment there was nothing. Then a voice, whispering. A child's, he thought at first. Some kid making prank calls, happening upon his number by accident.

"You think no one knows, don't you? You think no one knows what you did."

"Who is this?" He snapped the words, more sharply than he intended, and realized the faces around the table were turning toward him.

He shrugged, mouthing the words. *Wrong number.*

Then the whisperer spoke again. "You think no one knows about you and Josie. You think no one knows what you did. You're wrong. I know."

The connection was broken before he could say a word.

He glanced up. Everyone watched him. For an instant he imagined they'd all heard, that they all knew the truth about him.

Impossible. They watched him with varying degrees of interest, Jennifer with concern.

That look seemed to pierce the chill that had settled into his soul at the whispered words. The best thing that had come out of the reunion had been getting to know Jennifer again, feeling the warmth and caring that was such an integral part of her.

Don't kid yourself. Not even Jennifer would understand if she knew the truth.

The chill gripped again, harder. The truth—he'd struggled with it since the moment he'd learned that the body was Josie's. Struggled with what to do, how much to tell.

He'd thought the secret belonged to him alone. The voice seemed to whisper again. He'd been wrong.

Penny Brighton Kessler tossed the cell phone into the motel room's trash can, satisfied with the impression she'd made. She'd bought several phones this morning, inexpensive models that she could use and discard. No one would trace her that easily.

She crossed the worn carpeting to the window, peering around the edge of the drapery. Nothing suspicious in the ill-lit parking lot, but then, she'd been careful.

Were the police involved already? Probably—for the attack on Kate, at least. They couldn't have figured anything else out this soon. Unless she'd told Kate… She frowned. What had she told Kate?

Well, that didn't matter. She could deny everything Kate said. But it had all gone wrong. She'd thought her plan to lay the blame on Parker was perfect, but it had unraveled. And then Kate had taken one look at the photograph of Alexis and known she was Josie's child.

Anger propelled Penny back across the narrow room. Fine place this was for a Brighton—holed up in a cheap hotel room, on the run from the police, instead of living the life of luxury that was hers by right.

There were so many people to blame that she didn't know where to start. Her parents. The child she'd thought would guarantee her proper place in the world. All those self-righteous people from school. If they'd never gotten together again at that reunion, would any of this have happened?

Still, she'd known all along that things might turn sour. She'd taken what precautions she could. There was the car no one would trace to Penny Brighton Kessler, the change in her appearance. She ruffled her fingers through short curls. She'd always wondered what she'd look like as a redhead.

Cash was the problem. The amount she'd had hidden away wasn't enough. It wouldn't get her out of the country, or set her up properly in the way she ought to live.

The anger burned again—sharper, more focused now. Mason Grant had money. And Mason was as responsible as anyone. Ten years ago he'd ignored her and then had an affair with Josie, as stupid as she was naive.

Well, it was time Mason repaid her for taking care of his kid all these years. And if she could arrange for that, and hurt interfering Jennifer Pappas in the process, so much the better. If Jennifer hadn't tipped Kate and Parker off to her—

If, if, if. She forced down the fury that threatened to

choke her. She couldn't let it get the better of her. No more acting on impulse. She'd plan this carefully, and this time she'd wind up set for life.

The child was the key. Her parents had cut her off without a cent, but they loved Alexis, and would love her even when they knew she wasn't really their grandchild. She'd never get her hands on the trust fund they'd talked of setting up for Alexis, not when she was on the run, but if dear old Momma and Daddy thought Alexis was in danger, they'd come up with the cash.

And Mason? Well, she had to admit that he was the unknown factor in all of this. Would he go straight to the police? Or would he try to keep his secret?

If so, he should be willing enough to pay for the privilege. And if not, if he had some bizarre idea of being a father to the child he'd never known about, so much the better. If she controlled Alexis, they'd all dance to her tune.

She wanted to move. Act. Drive to that expensive boarding school where her parents kept the kid and take her away.

Too dangerous. The police could be watching the school, thinking she'd do just that.

She had to be patient. She'd start laying the groundwork—show Mason just how much he had to lose if he didn't cooperate with her.

He was vulnerable in spite of his wealth, in spite of the chain of sporting-goods stores that bore his name. The child, his precious reputation, the attachment he'd been forming with Jennifer since the reunion, these were his weaknesses.

She'd make him pay. The taste of revenge was sweet in her mouth. She'd make them all pay before she was done.

THREE

Jennifer checked the supplies in the art room for the after-school program in the church education wing, trying to focus on something other than the news about Penny and the child who might be Josie's. And on Mason's reaction to that news.

It was no use. She'd just counted the stacks of construction paper four times, and the amount still hadn't registered. She may as well give in to the temptation to speculate on the news like everyone else.

They'd all been upset. After all, their little group had known Penny and Josie better than most people. Despite the police's attempt at discretion, rumors were all over town, most of them garbled versions of what they'd heard at the pizzeria.

Everyone was upset. So why did Mason's reaction bother her?

The classroom door opened, and Pastor Rogers poked his head in. "Am I disturbing you?"

She smiled. "Not unless counting construction paper is more important than I think it is. Come in."

"I won't be a minute. Is everything going all right?" Robert Rogers gave her the warm, interested smile that drew people to Magnolia Christian Church and kept them coming back again and again. Showing Christ's love wasn't just a credo to Rob Rogers; it was an all-encompassing way of life.

"I'm doing fine, thanks to your willingness to give me a chance."

Affection for the big, burly minister warmed her heart. He hadn't changed much in ten years—maybe another gray hair or two, maybe an extra pound or so around the middle, that was all.

He shook his head. "You're an asset to the staff, Jennifer. I knew you would be. You don't have to keep thanking me for doing something that was good for all of us."

She flushed slightly. The praise was welcome, but they both knew that he'd taken a chance in hiring her. Other people might not be as quick to accept her innocence as he had been.

"Well, I just wanted to see—" He started to turn away, then turned back, slapping his head. "Honestly, I'll have to start putting sticky notes on my sleeve. I came down here to tell you that Mason Grant called. He's on his way over with some equipment he said he's donating to the after-school program."

"That's great." She'd see Mason, and she'd realize that there was nothing unusual about his reaction.

"I told him you'd meet him at the gym door. I hope that's okay." He beamed. "I'm sure we have you to thank for this donation. Mason hasn't shown any interest in the program in the past."

She shrugged. "I asked him, that was all. I'm sure he'd have responded the same way to anyone else from the church."

Or was she? Mason's faith, or lack of it, was a mystery to her, like so much else about his life.

"Must go." Pastor Rob raised his hand in a gesture vaguely reminiscent of a benediction. "I have a worship committee meeting and I'm probably late already." He hurried out, perpetually late but always forgiven because people knew that when he was there, they had his undivided love and attention.

She gave the room another glance. It wasn't easy to make the switch from the preschoolers who occupied it in the morning's nursery school to the elementary and middle school kids who swarmed in for the after-school program, but she and her volunteers had it down to an art by this time.

She hurried out into the hallway, passing the colorful murals she'd added to the cement block walls. Fanciful animals, two by two, marched all the way down one wall, headed for the ark at the end where Noah waited for them. On the opposite side, images of Jesus's miracles filled in the walls between the classroom doors.

The gym was in the basement of the old education building, which had been replaced in the fifties by the cement block building in which the nursery school was housed. The link between the two, on this level, involved pushing open a heavy fire door, passing through the low-ceilinged janitor's room with its doors into a maze of even older sections of the church's underpinnings, and spurting out into the teen lounge and then into the gym.

Mason would come to the door closest to the driveway, no doubt. She went to unlock it, her footfalls echoing hollowly on the bare wooden floor.

Funny. She was usually alone on this basement floor from the time the nursery school ended until the afterschool crew came charging in. She'd never before felt this urge to look behind her.

She shrugged, trying to shake off the tension that prickled along the nape of her neck. She'd been thinking too much about Josie, lying in a makeshift grave all those years when people thought she was living happily in Europe.

And about Penny. Kate thought Penny might come after her, the way she had everyone else who'd been involved with the class website. She shrugged that off. Once Josie's body had been found, everything was bound to come out. Her connecting the dots through the website was a minor part in solving the mystery.

Mason probably felt that empathy for poor Josie, too. That was why he'd reacted with such tension to Kate's news the previous night. There was nothing else to it.

She stood by the door, staring out the small window at the driveway. The gray stone walls of the sanctuary and the old education wing loomed over the drive on either side, turning it into a shadowed tunnel with the afternoon sunshine a gentle glow at the far end. Somewhere a door fell with a soft thud, and then the silence took over again.

She'd been back in Magnolia Falls for nearly a year

now. The job was going well, and she had a sense of accomplishment with what the Lord had allowed her to do here. She'd renewed cherished friendships with people she cared about, including Mason.

Especially Mason if she were being honest with herself. But she still wasn't sure what he felt, if anything, for her. He seemed to enjoy spending time with her, but she had yet to see behind the pleasant facade he presented to the world.

A white panel truck with the Grant's Sporting Goods logo on its side pulled into the driveway, turning almost gray in the deep shadows. Mason drew up, made a neat three-point turn and backed up to the gymnasium door. He slid out, walking with easy, athletic grace to the rear of the van.

She pushed open the heavy door and propped it with the wooden wedge that was always left handy. "Hi! I thought you'd come in this way." She scurried up the four steps to ground level. "I'll help you carry things in. This is so nice of you."

He passed her a cardboard carton and then pulled out two more to carry himself, giving her the slightly crooked smile that had a way of melting her heart. "As if I had a choice about it," he said.

"You did," she protested, remembering what Pastor Rob had said about it. "All I did was ask if you had any sports equipment you could donate. You could have said no."

He followed her back down the stairs and into the gym. "Like you'd have taken no for an answer." His voice was light and teasing, the tension of the previous night vanished. "You'd have pestered me to death if I hadn't agreed."

"Well, you belong to the church. Naturally I assume you want to support it."

"Naturally." There was a dry note to his voice that she didn't miss. "As it happens, my check to the church arrives promptly every week."

"You might bring it instead of mailing it," she ventured.

"I might," he said, his tone noncommittal.

What happened to him, Father? He was so devoted back in college, when we were in Campus Christian Fellowship together. Something has gone very wrong for him, and I don't know what. If I can help him, please show me the way.

She put the carton down on the gym floor and hesitated, longing to rip it open. "Can I see what's in here?"

Mason's eyebrows lifted. "There are more in the van. Don't you want to bring them all in first?"

"I want to see." She suspected she sounded like one of her four-year-olds.

He planted his hands on his hips, smiling at her. A shaft of sunlight, piercing through one of the high windows, turned his hair to burnished gold. "You were one of those kids who ripped open the birthday present before you looked to see who it was from, weren't you?"

"Guilty," she confessed. "Please?"

He shrugged. "Knock yourself out. It's just some basketballs, that's all. I have new baskets in one of the boxes, too. Those old things are so bent it's a wonder a ball can get through them." He nodded toward the existing baskets, which drooped dispiritedly from their worn backboards.

"They've probably been up there for thirty or forty years," she commented, eagerly ripping the box open. "This is so great. The kids will be thrilled."

The box held half a dozen basketballs, brand-new. She took one out and tossed it to him.

He caught it automatically, but then threw it back into the box with a quick thrust of his hands.

"Come on," she said invitingly, picking up the ball again. "Show me that hook shot of yours."

"Sorry. I don't play anymore." He turned and walked toward the door.

She paused, watching his lithe figure. No, she didn't understand what was going on with Mason. Maybe she never would.

She went to the van after him, helping to carry in another load of boxes, which proved to contain a couple of table-tennis sets.

"I can't thank you enough for this." She knew that sounded stilted, but she couldn't seem to help it. She sat down on the floor beside the boxes. "If you have work to do, I can unpack everything myself."

He stood for a moment, looking down at her, and then squatted next to her. "Don't be so polite, Miss Jennifer. Isn't that what the children call you?"

"It is. How did you know?" *Don't let me make a mistake and drive him away again.*

"I have my sources." He opened a box containing a wooden hockey game and started to put it together, his hands deft. "Look—about the basketball. I'm sorry if I was rude. I just don't like reminders of my failures, that's all."

She'd tell him he was overreacting, but she'd already

tried that, and it hadn't worked. "It must be tough to avoid an entire sport, in your line of work."

"Yeah, well, when you inherit the family business, you don't exactly have a lot of choices."

"I guess not. I just—" She looked at him, troubled.

"You want to make it better." He gave her a wry smile that twisted her heart. "You always want to make things better, don't you, Jennifer? Some things about people don't change."

"Some things do." She shivered a little. "Everything that's been coming out, about Josie, I mean, has me feeling as if the college days I thought I remembered might not have been real."

His face went still, and she couldn't tell what lay behind that stillness. "Maybe all our memories are a little skewed," he said finally. "We see what happened through our own perspective."

"Some things are simply true," she protested. "Our viewpoint doesn't change that. Josie's pregnancy—"

She stopped. She hadn't intended to bring that up.

"What about it?" His voice was even, his face bent over his work, a strand of blond hair falling onto his forehead.

"Well, she must have been pregnant in the spring of our senior year. She must have been upset, worried, trying to figure out what to do. I saw her every day. Why didn't I realize something was wrong?"

"She didn't want you to," he said. "You can't help everyone, Jennifer. Some people won't let you." It sounded very final. He lifted the hockey game and propped it against the wall. "There you are, all finished. Anything else I can do for you?"

He rose as he spoke, holding out his hand. She grasped it, and he pulled her effortlessly to her feet. For an instant she felt dizzy. Her eyes met his—met and held. Her breath stopped. Mason didn't move. Even the dust motes floating in the shaft of sunlight seemed still.

"You— What did you say?" Her voice sounded unnatural to her.

He blinked, as if trying to refocus. "I asked if I could do anything else for you."

You could open up to me. You could explain what just happened.

"Nothing, unless you'd like to come in and show the children how to use all this equipment. We're always looking for volunteers." That was better. Her voice sounded almost normal.

"I'm afraid you'll have to keep looking. I'm no good with kids." His face seemed to tense on the words.

"You never know until you try," she said. *Open up to me, Mason. Talk to me.*

"I don't think so. I'll see you, Jennifer." He walked out quickly, as if to deny that anything at all had just happened between them.

Mason sat at his desk a couple of days later, trying to concentrate on the latest sales reports from the Macon store. Concentrating was never easy with the massive oil painting of his father mounted on the wall above, staring down at him. It seemed to be reminding him that it was Gerald Grant II who was supposed to be sitting in that chair, not Mason.

Small wonder he preferred to work anywhere but here. He could move the portrait, of course. He toyed with that thought for a moment, even knowing it was impossible. Think how scandalized Eva Morrissey would be if he did such a thing.

He'd inherited Eva, his father's secretary, when he inherited the business, and their working relationship had been set at a time when he'd been too young and too insecure to take a firm line with her. As a result, she felt free to criticize everything he did, including that donation to the after-school program.

Suspicious, that had been the only word for her attitude. Why would he want to do something like that? He never had before. His father never had.

That was the gold standard for Eva. What would his father have done?

Maybe that was all the more reason to make the donation. He shoved his chair back from the computer, stretching. But that wasn't why he'd given the equipment. He knew perfectly well why. Because Jennifer had asked him to do it.

Well, so what? It was natural enough. Friends supported each other's interests.

That sentiment was something that wouldn't have occurred to him before the reunion. Then, he'd preferred not to move too deeply into friendships or romantic relationships. He'd kept his personal life on the surface. It was much safer that way.

Getting back in touch with the gang from college had begun to change his attitude. It had forced him to remember that guy he used to be. That kid had been naive, maybe. Guilty of a lot of mistakes. But at least he'd had some humanity.

Not entirely comfortable with the direction his thoughts were taking, he shoved his chair back and moved to one of the wide windows that looked down on Main Street. This had been his father's office, and his father had liked overlooking what he considered his domain.

The warm spring day had brought the college students downtown in force. They sauntered along the sidewalks in groups and couples, underneath the banners mounted on light standards in navy and gold, Magnolia College colors. Where would their downtown be without the college to give it life, to say nothing of business?

He could remember being one of those kids, headed for a quick slice of Burt's pizza or a serious talk about the nature of the universe over a cup of coffee at the Half Joe. Even now, Burt stood in the doorway of the pizza shop, his white apron pristine, surveying the downtown scene as he'd been doing for years.

A couple walked past Burt, arms linked, heads together, so absorbed in each other that the rest of the world might not exist. Burt watched them tolerantly. He'd seen young love plenty of times before.

Mason drew back from the window slightly, remembering those moments with Jennifer in the church gym. The attraction had been strong. He couldn't deny that. Jennifer had recognized it, too. He'd seen it in the way her brown eyes widened, the way her generous mouth softened.

It was no good, of course. Jennifer wasn't remotely

like the women he usually dated. She'd want something real in a relationship, and he didn't have anything real to give.

The door opened behind him, and he swung around, frowning. That was one of Eva's more annoying traits, bursting in on him as if she hoped she might catch him napping or playing solitaire on the computer instead of working.

Now her eyes, sharp behind her old-fashioned half-glasses, swept the office before coming to rest on him. "Miss Pappas is here to see you. I told her you were working." She made the words sound accusing.

Ignoring her, he strode across the office and pulled the door wide. Jennifer stood there, looking a little hesitant after hearing Eva's greeting. Her glossy black hair was pulled back into a single braid, and she wore the khakis and cotton top that seemed to be her working uniform.

"Jennifer, please come in." He gave Eva a pointed stare. "Thank you, Eva."

She had no choice but to retreat, but she shot Jennifer a suspicious glance as she closed the door behind her.

"Don't mind Eva. She's universally rude." He guided her to the leather visitor's chair and perched on the desk. "It's nice to see you."

The conventional words were truer than he wanted to admit. He reminded himself of all the reasons why anything other than friendship wouldn't work between them.

"I hope you don't mind my stopping by. I didn't mean to interrupt your work."

"Believe it or not, and I sometimes have trouble believing it myself, I'm the boss here. I get to take a break whenever I want. How are the kids enjoying the sports gear?"

A smile blossomed on her face. "They're delighted. Actually, that's why I came. They sent you something." She reached into the oversized bag she carried and pulled out a sheet of newsprint. "This is for you."

He unfolded it to find colorful crayoned images of kids shooting hoops and playing with the hockey set. Slightly crooked cursive letters proclaimed their thanks for his generosity.

The childlike simplicity of the picture touched him more than he'd liked to admit, even though he realized that Jennifer had probably engineered their thanks.

"It's great. Thanks for bringing it." She could have mailed it, of course, but she hadn't.

"I had to come downtown to the print shop anyway." She seemed to read his thoughts. "And there was something else that belongs to you." She handed him a business-sized envelope.

"If this is a thank-you from Pastor Rob, you can tell everyone to stop thanking me." He ripped the envelope open. "It makes me feel as if the world is surprised that I could be generous."

"No, it's not that. I mean—"

He flipped open the single page. His obviously shocked expression cut off her words.

It took a couple of seconds to comprehend what he was looking at. The sheet was a copy of one of the store's print ads—the one with a photo of him that the advertising director had talked him into. An exact duplicate, except that someone had changed the text.

Instead of the usual invitation to visit the store's semiannual sale, the ad had another message. *Come in and meet Josie Skerritt's secret lover.*

The taunt seared his soul. He crumpled the page with an involuntary spasm of his fingers.

"Where did you get this?" His voice was so harsh it didn't sound like his.

Jennifer drew back at the accusation in his tone, her eyes wide, her hands braced on the arms of the chair as if she wanted to flee. "Mason, what's wrong? What is it?"

He took a breath, forcing himself back under control. "This letter. Where did it come from?"

"It came to the church office. Look at it. You'll see." She nodded toward the envelope, which had fluttered to lie facedown, a white rectangle against the dark blue carpet.

He bent, scooping it up, and flipped it over.

"You see." Jennifer leaned toward him. "It came in this morning's mail. It has your name on it, but the church address. We couldn't imagine why anyone would send it that way, but I said I'd drop it off, since I was coming by anyway."

He frowned at the envelope. It was addressed exactly as she'd said, in block letters printed in black ink. There was no return address. The postmark read Savannah, Georgia. Nothing to indicate who had sent it, and so many people had undoubtedly handled it that fingerprints would be useless.

Who could it be but the person who'd made that call

to his cell phone, taunting him? Penny? That seemed the obvious choice.

But to what end? If she had sent it, what could she possibly hope to gain?

He looked at Jennifer, assessing her. She couldn't have read the note, but she obviously knew he was upset. He could see nothing in her face but concern.

Still, why had the letter gone to the church? And was the fact that it ended up in Jennifer's hands merely a coincidence?

FOUR

"Thanks so much, but I couldn't possibly eat another bite." Jennifer shook her head at the slice of moist, rich applesauce cake Kate held out temptingly. "I just wanted to talk. You didn't really have to feed me, but it's delicious."

Kate put the slice of cake back on the platter, smiling. "Brandon will eat it. That boy will eat anything. And I have to confess—I didn't make the cake. Parker did."

"You and Parker are getting to be quite an item, aren't you?" She hadn't come to talk about Kate's romance, but she just couldn't resist. The love between the two of them when they were together would make anyone's heart warm.

Even at the mention of his name, Kate's eyes grew soft. "You could say that. You know where he is tonight? Taking Brandon to a scout meeting. Can you imagine how rare it is to find a man who cares that much for my son?"

"You're lucky." Her voice softened. Was she ever going to be that fortunate?

"Funny." Kate picked up her coffee cup and held it between her hands, her blue eyes seeming to look off into the distance. "How much we've changed since college. I have, anyway. I want completely different things now than I did then."

"No big career in music now?" She remembered Kate's dream of making it in Nashville. And really, she'd seemed to have every chance at success, with her beauty, talent and drive.

"I wouldn't have it on a silver platter." The answer was emphatic. "I just want my family and my nursing, and I'll be happy."

"I'm glad for you, Kate. And for Parker. You're going to be great together."

"We are." Kate took a sip of the coffee, and her expression turned brisk. "But come on, now. You didn't come out in the rain tonight just to eat Parker's applesauce cake and hear me being sappy about my love. What's on your mind?"

Jennifer smiled. She could just see Kate, running a hospital ward with brisk efficiency. The most popular girl on campus had found her place in life.

"You caught me. I wondered if you'd found out any more about what's happening with Penny. And that poor little girl. Have they proven yet if she's really Josie's daughter?"

"I'm not exactly in the police's confidence." Kate made a face. "In fact, I think they'd like it if we'd all butt out of official business. But I think they are trying to locate her and get a warrant for DNA testing."

"But don't you think it's odd that none of us guessed Josie was pregnant that spring semester? We were all in Edith Sutton Hall together."

"Good old Edith Sutton. Long on Southern charm, short on amenities. I'm certainly glad I'm not living there any longer." Kate glanced with satisfaction around her spotless kitchen, done in subtle earth tones. "But really, is it so surprising? Senior year we had private rooms, so it's not as if anyone was with her twenty-four hours a day."

"Even so, you'd think we would have noticed something. All those nights when we sat around the lounge and talked until one in the morning, all those warm evenings when we went up on the roof." It came back so vividly—the scent of jasmine in the air, the soft sounds of the women's voices confiding secrets in the dark. "You'd think she'd have said something."

"Well, I don't know about you, but I was totally preoccupied that semester with what I was going to do after graduation. I was probably too self-centered to notice anyone else's trouble." Kate sounded almost amused at the girl she'd been.

"Not self-centered," Jennifer protested. "Just busy."

"Well, you were, too. As I recall, you went home every weekend to help take care of your mother. I was sorry to hear about her death, by the way. I don't know that I ever told you that."

Jennifer nodded, her throat tight. Her mother had made a gallant effort to live a normal life despite her multiple sclerosis. "She insisted I live on campus that semester. She didn't want to deprive me of that experience, even though they could have used me at home."

"Mothers have a habit of wanting the best for their children," Kate said. "I don't think I really understood that until I was a mother myself."

"I suppose it's possible Josie thought she was doing what was best for her child. Maybe she intended to give the baby up for adoption." She thought about what Mason had said—that Josie hadn't wanted them to know, hadn't wanted their help. "Do you think she'd have come to one of us if she'd needed anything?"

Kate tilted her head to one side, considering. "Josie was always a bit of a mouse."

"She was quiet. So was I."

"That's different. You were warmhearted but shy, just like you are now. Josie—I don't know. She was quiet, as you say, but she could be as stubborn as a mule laying back its ears."

That startled Jennifer into a laugh. "I guess so. Remember when she was determined to challenge you for the solo at the Christmas choral concert? Everyone knew you were the better singer, but she wouldn't leave it alone."

"I remember that I got obsessed about it, too," Kate said dryly. "Not very becoming for the Christian I professed to be."

"I guess we were all baby Christians then, for all we thought we knew." She reached out impulsively to touch Kate's hand. "I'm sure you've thought about it. Do you have any idea who the father could have been?"

Kate shook her head slowly. "I've been over it and over it, especially when the police were so sure it was Parker. I just don't remember Josie even dating anyone that winter. She was friends with Penny, of course, but Penny was never really involved with the rest of us. For the most part, the gang of us from CCF just hung out together instead of pairing off."

"I wish—" She stopped and shook her head. "It's foolish to wish to change the past. But I'd like to think I'd been kind to Josie when she was going through all that."

Kate nodded. "I know what you mean. It gets to me to know that all these years she's been lying there alone."

"Same here. But she wasn't really there. And not really alone." She blinked back tears. "Would it be awkward if I asked you to pray for her with me?"

"It would be very right." Kate's hand clasped hers, and she bowed her head.

Jennifer took a breath, and the words seemed to form in her heart. "Dear Father, we hold up to You our sister, Josie. We know she's safe in Your hands now, and we ask You to bring her peace."

"And forgive us, Father, for any chance we missed to show her love and kindness." Kate's voice was husky. "Amen."

Jennifer squeezed her hand before releasing it. "I don't know that we solved anything tonight, but I have to say I feel better."

"I do, too." Kate wiped away an errant tear. "Goodness, I haven't cried in I don't know how long. Maybe I'd better eat another piece of cake."

Jennifer laughed, shoving her chair back. "You do that. Cake is definitely comfort food. I'd better get going or Dad will be worried. He hates it when I drive at night in the rain in that old clunker of mine."

"Come back anytime." Kate gave her a quick hug. "I can't promise it will be this quiet, but I'd love to have you here."

She nodded, opening the door. A gust of wind blew

a spray of rain into her face, and she fought to get her umbrella up. "I'm going to run for it. Good night."

She raced toward her car, getting soaked but unable to do anything about it, and then fought to get the umbrella down. She'd probably have been better off without it.

Thankfully she slammed the door on the rain and reached for the ignition. A hot shower and a change of clothes would feel good when she got home. Kate's charming cottage was near the campus, so it was a good five miles to the house in the country Dad had insisted was his perfect retirement place. Her things would be clammy by then.

It didn't take long to get out of Magnolia Falls, no matter where you were. She was clear of town in a few minutes and onto the narrow county road that led home. Unfortunately the rain showed no sign of lessening. It beat on the windshield relentlessly, with her wipers struggling unsuccessfully to keep up.

She slowed, mindful of the swamp that bordered the road on the right, and squinted. The rain reflected her headlight beams back at her from the black macadam, and she could barely see the edge of the road.

Not much farther, in any event. She'd be home soon, and that hot shower was waiting. She shivered as the damp fabric of her slacks clung to her legs, and she turned the heater on. The windshield fogged up instantly, and she switched it back off again. She'd rather see than be warm. Only a couple more miles—

The engine sputtered, coughed once and died. She glided slowly to a stop, steering to the edge of the road, but not daring to pull off when she couldn't see what the surface was like.

She pounded her fist lightly on the steering wheel. Dad kept offering to buy her a newer car, but she'd stubbornly stuck to her decision to wait until she could afford it herself.

She'd had a decent savings account once, before the cost of defending herself wiped it out. No one ever mentioned that even the innocent had to pay.

She tried the ignition key again. The electrical system was okay, so what—then she saw the gas gauge, sitting uncompromisingly on empty.

How could she be out of gas? The only thing her little car had going for it was it got good gas mileage. It couldn't have used a half a tank going from church to home to Kate's.

A chill crept along the back of her neck. Not unless someone tampered with it.

Shaking off the thought, she grabbed her bag and pulled out the cell phone. She'd worry about how later. Right now she'd call Dad—

A car rounded the bend, coming toward her, and pulled up directly in front of her, its headlights blinding her eyes so that she couldn't see anything else.

Her heart thudded, deafening her. Think, don't panic. Check the door locks. Call for help.

Even as she fumbled for the cell phone buttons, it rang. Shaken, she answered.

"Get out of the car." A woman's voice commanded in a Southern accent.

"No. What do you want? Who are you?" *Please, Lord,*

protect me. She squinted, trying to make out the color of the car, the shape behind the windshield.

"Why, Jennifer, don't you recognize your old college friend?" The voice was taunting. "It's Penny. I just want to talk. Get out of the car, and we'll reminisce about old times."

"No." Penny might be crazy, but she wasn't. "Leave me alone."

"Not willing to get out? But I want to be able to see your face. Still, I guess I can manage that." Another light came on, this one shining full in her face, so bright she put up her hand to shield her eyes. A deer-spotting light, she realized. And she was the deer.

She wasn't helpless. She might not be able to move, but she could cut the connection, dial 9-1-1—

"Now, don't be stubborn, Jennifer. You can help my daughter, Alexis. That's what you're all about, isn't it? Helping kids?"

How did she know that? How did Penny know anything about her? She hesitated, pressing the phone close to her ear. "Don't you mean Josie's daughter?"

"Now, you don't want to irritate me." Penny's voice went soft with venom. "I just might be tempted to push your little car right off the road and into the swamp if you do."

Jennifer clenched her teeth. Could she? Would she? She really didn't want to find out. "Tell me what you want and leave me alone."

"I suppose I must if you won't walk down memory lane with me. It's very simple, really." Penny sounded satisfied that she was going to get what she wanted. "I want you to carry a message to Alexis's father. Tell him that for a hundred thousand, I'll keep quiet about him. No one else needs to know he's the father. I'll get in touch with you to tell him how to deliver it."

She shook her head, trying to make sense of this. "Who? Who are you talking about? I don't know who the child's father is."

For a moment the cell phone was silent. Then Penny laughed softly, and dread pooled in Jennifer's heart.

"You know, don't you? You've figured it out. Alexis's father is your good friend. Mason Grant."

FIVE

Mason had always considered his home a sanctuary, and he'd never needed it as much as he did right now. He sank down in the leather armchair, propping his feet on the hassock, and leaned back. Little about the house was traditional, and that was the way he liked it. The great room combined kitchen, dining area, media room and library into one flowing, harmonious whole.

He'd started a fire in the stone fireplace when he got home—not that it was that chilly, but the blaze seemed to take away some of the dampness from the teeming rain. The storm was a real frog-choker, as the old-timers liked to say, turning the red clay soil into a quagmire.

Now he stared into the flames, willing himself to think of anything but the events of the past few days. From the rough-hewn timber that formed his mantel a picture faced him—one of the few things he'd brought from the overdecorated antebellum mansion that his parents had called home.

Two young faces smiled out of the frame. A fishing trip, far up the reaches of the Ogeechee. Twelve years old, he'd been, and proud beyond measure that his eighteen-year-old big brother had agreed to take him. He held up the striped bass he'd caught, grinning from ear to ear in the classic fisherman's pose.

Gerry had probably been bored to tears, but he hadn't shown it. He'd always been kind to his kid brother, maybe aware of the obvious favoritism their parents, especially Dad, showed to him.

Well, why wouldn't Gerry be the favorite? He'd been the original All-American kid, good at everything, a son to make his parents proud.

At eighteen, he'd had the world by the tail—graduating first in his class, voted most popular boy, riding the wave of a state championship basketball team and a full scholarship to Duke.

A month later he'd been dead. All that promise gone in a moment's miscalculation, a single bad decision. And life had never been the same for those he left behind.

The buzz of the doorbell jerked his mind away from old grief, jolting his nerves with the possibility of trouble to come. The police? It wouldn't surprise him.

He went to the door and opened it. It wasn't the cops. It was Jennifer, standing on his porch, soaking wet, her eyes huge, her strained face white.

"Jennifer." He seized her arm, pulled her inside when she seemed incapable of moving. "You're soaked to the skin. What are you doing out on a night like this?"

"I had to see you." She shivered, the movement quaking her slender frame to her toes. "We have to talk."

"Whatever it is, it can wait until we get you dry." He'd never seen calm, self-possessed Jennifer look this way, and it shook him. "Let me get a towel—"

He started to turn away, but she grabbed his arm, her fingers wet and cold when they touched his skin. "I don't want a towel. I want to talk."

Something was wrong—very wrong.

He snatched a woven coverlet from the nearest chair and tossed it around her shoulders, then propelled her physically toward the fire. "All right, we'll talk." He smoothed the coverlet down over her arms. "At least try to get warm while we do."

She seemed oblivious of her physical surroundings, of everything except the need that flamed in her eyes. "Just tell me the truth. You had an affair with Josie, didn't you?"

The words hit him like a blow. He couldn't lie, not to Jennifer. But he didn't want to let the word come out of his mouth. "What makes you say that? Did someone accuse me?"

Were people talking already? That phony ad had been a threat, of course—a hint that the sender wouldn't hesitate to make his sins public.

"Just answer me!" Her fists clenched, her mouth twisted with the effort to hold back tears. "Tell me."

"Jennifer—don't. Don't care so much." He felt as if he were being wrung by a giant hand. "Yes, it's true. Josie and I were intimate. Once. That's all. Just once."

But once was enough, obviously. Did God calculate your sins by the number?

"You kept silent." That was disbelief in her eyes.

"All this time, while everyone has been wondering who fathered Josie's baby—"

"It could have been me. Yes." A sudden burst of anger swept through him. Who was Jennifer to judge him in that way? "When they identified the body as Josie's and said she'd had a child, of course I thought of the possibility, but it seemed so unlikely. We were together only once, we'd used protection—"

He stopped, the anger seeping away. "Excuses, that's all those are. I never should have let it happen. It was my fault. But can't you understand that I wasn't eager to publish my sins to the world? Or set myself up to be suspect number one with the police?"

"The police." There was something in her gaze—something hurt and wary and almost knowing—that confused him. "I guess I can understand that. You were trying to protect yourself."

It sounded pretty selfish, put that way. Still, how else could it be put? Jennifer, even with her soft heart, wasn't one to falsify the truth to make him feel better. She was far more likely to quietly insist that he face it, whatever it was.

The tension left her, so abruptly that he could see it happen, and she sank into the nearest chair. "That's it, then. I knew you were hiding something."

He pulled a chair up and sat down opposite her, close, so that they were knee to knee. "We all hide things, don't we? Tell me what brought you here tonight. Did you just guess at the truth?"

She shook her head, looking suddenly drained. "She told me."

"She—who?" All his senses went on alert. "Jennifer, tell me what's going on."

"Penny. Penny told me."

Penny? Shock rippled through him. "How could you find out from Penny? She's on the run—the police figure far away from here by now."

"Well, they're wrong," she said flatly. She leaned her head on her palm, as if too weary to keep holding it up. "I saw her— Well, didn't see, exactly. But she was there."

This wasn't making a whole lot of sense. He leaned forward and clasped both her hands in his. "Tell it from the beginning. Where were you tonight?"

She nodded like an obedient child, staring down at the Berber carpet. "I'd gone over to Kate's this evening. To talk. You know where she lives—the cottage over near the campus?"

"Yes."

"I started driving home, out the old county road toward Fisherdale. I didn't get there. I ran out of gas." She looked up then, eyes wide. "She'd siphoned the gas out of my tank. While Kate and I were in the kitchen, she was out in the dark, watching us. Afterwards she told me. She'd left it in a can in the trunk of my car. So I could get here, to tell you."

It sounded totally improbable, but obviously there was more to come. "You were stuck out there on the road. Did you call for help?"

"I started to. But a car came. It pulled up nose-to-nose with mine. And then my cell phone rang. It was her. Penny. She wanted me to get out of the car and talk to her." He felt her shiver through their clasped hands. "I wouldn't get out."

"Thank Heaven." Penny was dangerous. She'd attacked Kate, stolen Josie's baby, probably killed Josie. Fear clawed at his heart at the thought of Jennifer alone with her.

"She threatened to push my car into the swamp if I didn't listen to her."

"What did she want? Surely not just to spill the truth about me."

"She wanted me to deliver a message." Jennifer pulled back, drawing her hands free, looking at him steadily. "To you, because she said you're Alexis's father. She said if you pay her a hundred thousand dollars, she won't tell anyone."

He certainly hadn't foreseen this. He struggled to process it all. "I suppose she needs the money to get out of the country before the police catch up to her. So Penny believes I'm the father. Or she pretends to believe it, because I'm the most likely candidate to have that kind of money and be willing to pay her off."

"Aren't you? Will you give her the money to keep quiet?" Anger flicked the words. "That's what you want, isn't it? To deny that you might be that little girl's father?"

He leaned back, carefully not touching her. It hurt to see the scorn in Jennifer's eyes.

"I won't pay off Penny unless that's what the police want me to do. I've already told them everything, Jennifer. I might be a jerk, but I'm not bad enough to continue to deny it once the child was found. They're running a DNA test. We'll know soon enough if I'm the father of Josie's baby."

Jennifer sank back in the chair, clutching the coverlet around her. The adrenaline that had kept her going since the encounter with Penny vanished, leaving her shaken and weak.

Mason and Josie. Josie's baby. It hurt more than it should, to think of that.

She was vaguely aware of Mason, watching her with a worried expression. She had to get a hold of herself. She shouldn't betray her feelings so readily to him.

He moved suddenly. "You need something to warm you up. I'll get some coffee. Do you want me to call anyone? Kate? Your dad?"

"No, I'm all right." She forced a smile. "Coffee would be good, though." Maybe it would help her stop shaking inside.

Mason walked quickly across the spacious living area and around the breakfast bar into the kitchen, looking unexpectedly domestic as he busied himself with the coffeepot and cups.

If Josie had lived, would they be married now? Would this be Josie's home, hers and Mason's and their daughter's? Somehow she couldn't get her mind around that picture.

Mason had been her friend in college, nothing more. If she'd ever wished for another kind of relationship with him—well, she'd known he wasn't for her, and she'd tried to be happy with friendship.

She'd always thought she knew him as well as she

knew anyone, better maybe. But she'd never even dreamed of him with Josie. Didn't want to imagine it even now, she realized.

She was being ridiculous. She hadn't seen Mason in ten years, until the reunion brought them all back together again. Since then, their friendship had been a casual thing, with never a word or gesture from Mason to hint that he wanted anything more.

People changed in ten years. She had. How could she know the man he was now, when she obviously hadn't really known the boy he was back in college?

He came back quickly, carrying a tray with two thick white mugs, creamer and sugar, a small plate containing a few biscotti. "Luckily I already had the coffee on. And they say sugar is good for shock."

"I'm not hungry." But it was easier to take biscotti with her coffee than to have him watching her with that worried look.

Only when she had begun to sip the hot brew did he serve himself, sitting down in the chair opposite her and holding the mug between his hands, as if he needed to warm up, too.

"The fire is nice." An inane comment, but probably better than the hurt questions she wanted to shoot at him. "And I like your house."

She glanced around the great room, warm and almost rustic with its exposed wood. The wide-planked floors were covered here and there with braided area rugs, and the couches and chairs were overstuffed leather.

At the side of the living area, glass doors led out onto a flagstone patio, where small lights showed a pot of tulips, a string hammock and a gas-powered grill. The scene invited one to what was clearly an outside living room.

"You mean, it's considerably different from the house I grew up in, don't you?"

She shrugged, remembering that chilly mansion where they'd had the Campus Christian Fellowship Christmas dinner once. "Well, I never really thought that place was decorated in your taste."

The Grant mansion had certainly been a far cry from the comfortable middle-class houses her family had lived in whenever her dad's job took them to a new town.

"This is a lot more comfortable. When my mother had to go into an assisted-living facility, selling that place seemed the best option." His face tightened slightly. "I'm afraid she's never become reconciled to that, although now she doesn't remember."

"I'm sorry. I didn't realize." Her mind flickered to her mother's long battle with MS. Dad had been a pillar of strength throughout, never questioning that she belonged at home, with them. Of course, Mason's father had died their senior year, so he wouldn't have had him to rely on. "A lot happened our senior year."

"Yes." He didn't seem to have any trouble following the progression of her thoughts. A muscle twitched in his jaw. "After my father died, I was thrown into trying to run the business and take care of my mother."

"And Josie?" The question was out before she considered that she didn't have the right to ask.

He shook his head. "I'm not proud of it. You must know that. But there was never anything between Josie and me but one night when we both had too much to drink and too many problems we wanted to forget. Afterward, she refused ever to talk about it. If the child is mine—— Well, she never told me."

"I'm sorry. I shouldn't have asked. I don't have the right to question you."

His tight expression eased a little. "Maybe you earned that right when Penny dragged you into the middle of this. I can't believe she's still hanging around Magnolia Falls with every cop in the state on the alert for her."

"You could be right. She needs money to get away, and she thinks this is a way of getting it." She wouldn't ask the question that nagged at her.

"I wouldn't pay her to keep it a secret." Again, he seemed to know what she was thinking. "But the police may want me to play along with her. This could help them catch her."

The police. She was hypersensitive, of course, after her past experience, but she could only be relieved that Mason was the one who had to deal with the police.

He set his coffee mug back on the tray. "I should probably call them now, if you feel well enough to talk with them."

"Me?" It came out too high-pitched. He'd know something was wrong. "I mean, why do I have to talk to them? Surely you can tell them everything they need to know."

His brows drew down in a frown. "Jennifer, you can't be serious. You were accosted by a woman who's wanted by the police—for assault, if not for murder. Of course they'll want to talk with you."

Of course they would. Her stomach churned, and

she felt as if the coffee were burning a hole in it. Thanks to Penny, she was about to become involved with the police again.

Having two police detectives in his living room didn't do a thing for the atmosphere, Mason decided. Still, it was undoubtedly better than trying to get Jennifer to go to the police station. She'd looked so panicked at the thought that he hadn't had the heart to keep insisting.

Nikki Rivers, the detective he'd initially spoken with when he'd decided it was time to reveal his involvement with Josie, sat next to Jennifer, leading her gently through her story.

Fortunately Rivers seemed to recognize that this had been a shocking experience. After all, Jennifer had been threatened by the woman who'd recently tried to kill her best friend. Kate had been fortunate to escape with nothing worse than a gunshot wound to the arm. The thought of Penny turning a gun on Jennifer knotted his stomach.

Rivers and Paterson, who stood leaning against the mantelpiece and listening intently, hadn't seen that panic in Jennifer's face at the suggestion of going to the police. By the time they arrived, she'd been composed.

He was the only one who'd seen it, and it still bothered him. It made him want to protect her, if he were honest with himself, even as he wondered why the prospect of talking to the police upset her so much.

Jennifer had gotten to the point of telling the police about Penny siphoning the gas from her car while she was at Kate's when she stopped, her brown eyes going wide. "Kate doesn't know about this. I should have called her. We have to warn her." She fumbled in her shoulder bag, probably for her cell phone.

Nikki Rivers put a restraining hand on hers. "It's all right, Miss Pappas. We've already called her about it, and another unit is over there right now."

Rivers looked as calm and composed as if they'd called her in the middle of a normal business day instead of late in the evening. Had she and Paterson been on duty, or had they been brought in because this connected up with Josie's death?

"I don't think the Brighton woman would go after her now, in any event," Paterson said. "It wouldn't do her any good."

Jennifer moved restlessly. "I'm not sure she's thinking that rationally."

Rivers shrugged. "Well, she's rational enough that she's out for the money that she thinks would let her get away."

"I wonder why—" Jennifer began, and then she stopped.

"What do you wonder, Miss Pappas?" Rivers's voice was gentle, but her gaze coolly assessed Jennifer's face.

"Well, everyone always thought Penny's family was quite well-off. I'm surprised she has to go to such extremes to get money."

Rivers exchanged glances with the other detective. Mason thought he saw a slight nod.

"We've been talking with the Brighton woman's parents, up in Charleston. Elderly folks, not in very good health. Apparently they became fed up with their daughter's actions some time ago. Cut her off, as we understand it, but continued to support the child, keeping her in an expensive boarding school on the outskirts of Atlanta and setting up a trust fund for her."

"Except that now it seems the child isn't Penny's at all." It took an effort for him to say the words without thinking about Josie lying in a makeshift grave.

Paterson nodded. "It's a strange one, I grant you. Her parents are in a state of shock. Still, they love the girl. I don't imagine they'll stop doing that."

"That poor child." Jennifer brushed a tendril of hair back from her face. "She's awfully young to be in a boarding school, I'd think."

"Under the circumstances, it's probably better than being with the Brighton woman," Rivers said. "And she sees the grandparents often, even if they're not able to have her on a full-time basis."

"You'll catch Penny, won't you?" Jennifer glanced from one detective to the other. "Now that you know she's still in the area, surely you'll be able to find her."

"We'll try." Rivers turned him. "But in the meantime, we need to know if you're willing to play along with her, assuming she contacts you, Mr. Grant."

"Yes, of course. Anything to get this settled."

"We'll want to put monitoring devices on your home and office phones."

He shrugged impatiently. "Fine."

Rivers turned to Jennifer. "And we'll need to do the same with your phones if you have no objection."

"Why Jennifer's phones?" He was startled into asking the question. "I'm the one Penny wants."

"She may feel safer using an intermediary." The detective sounded as patient as if she were explaining to a child. "That was probably in her mind tonight—that she'd find it simpler and safer to intimidate Miss Pappas than to take you on directly."

Maybe it seemed obvious to the cops, but all he knew was that he hated the thought of Jennifer being involved in this nightmare. "She might pick on any of my friends, in that case."

"She might, but she approached Miss Pappas this time." She looked at Jennifer with that cool, assessing gaze again. "Do you have any idea why?"

Jennifer shook her head. "We were never particularly close in college. I knew her, like I knew everyone in my class, but we weren't friends. I don't know why she'd pick on me, unless it was because I was involved with the class website. In a way, I suppose I put Kate onto her."

Rivers made a noncommittal sound. "You don't mind, then, if we monitor your calls?"

"No." But she didn't sound very happy about it. "But what if she does call? What should I do?"

"Agree to everything she says. Keep her on the phone as long as possible. We'll be tracing the call."

"Forget it." He couldn't stay out of it any longer. "Jennifer shouldn't be involved in this. If she's not available, Penny will have to come to me directly, won't she?"

"I don't know—" Rivers began.

"No, Mason. We can't take that chance." Jennifer sat very straight, her face pale and set. "This is too important. That little girl—we have to do everything we can to be sure Penny can't get anywhere near her again." She looked at Mason. "I have to do whatever I can."

SIX

Two days had passed, and Mason still wasn't reconciled to having Jennifer involved in this plan to trap Penny. Despite all the police assurances that she'd never be in any danger, he wasn't convinced.

He paced across the office to the window, staring down at the street for a moment, and then turned to glance at the clock on his desk. It wasn't quite time to meet Jennifer for lunch.

The truth was that she hadn't wanted to meet him at all. When he'd called her last night, she'd been too polite to come right out and say it. So he'd been persistent, and in the end, she'd agreed. That was Jennifer—always too soft-hearted for her own good.

Well, at the moment that had played to his advantage. She was meeting him, and he'd have a chance to try and talk her out of getting involved in this situation. Penny was his responsibility.

Was her reluctance to meet him a sign that she didn't think much of him after finding out about his affair with Josie? Probably so. His jaw tightened. That shouldn't matter to him, not if it helped convince her to stay out of this.

Still, it hurt to see the disappointment in her eyes when she looked at him. They'd been friends once, good friends. But he ought to be used to people being disappointed in him.

All the more reason why he didn't want to feel responsible for Jennifer's safety. Let Penny call him if she meant to go through with this. All Jennifer had to do was leave town for a few days, and Penny would have no choice.

Now if he could convince Jennifer of that. He glanced at his clock again. Finally it was time to leave. He walked quickly across to the door and on into the outer office where Eva reigned.

Eva Morrissey looked up from her computer, frowning at him over her glasses. "I didn't know you were going out today."

She was always convinced that she had the right to know where he was at all times. "I'm going to lunch. I'll be back in about an hour."

She glanced at the round wall clock that had been there since the building was built and Grant's Sporting Goods moved in. "It's late for lunch."

He kept a curb on his tongue. Eva had been upset enough by the visit from the police technician to work on the phones. The last thing he needed was to get into a quarrel over her insistence on knowing where he was at all times.

"I'll be back in about an hour," he repeated, and walked out.

The Half Joe Coffee Shop was across the street and

up a half block. He crossed Main Street, trying to focus on the beauty of the azaleas in full bloom along the front of the antique shop instead of the mess his personal life was in.

It didn't work. He couldn't keep his mind on anything else. Josie's child—maybe his child. Penny Brighton—a threat to all of them. And Jennifer, with her warm heart and her instinctive need to help.

He'd pray, but God didn't seem to listen to him anymore.

Take one step at a time. That was all he could do to get out of the convoluted maze in which he found himself. And that first step was to convince Jennifer to go away for a few days, putting herself out of range of Penny and her machinations.

Fifteen minutes later he'd begun to wonder if he'd even have a chance to try. He'd found a table at the back of the busy coffee shop, out of hearing range from the nearest cluster of students with their laptops and lattes. He nursed a black coffee, shaking his head at the waiter who kept wanting to take his order, and watched the windows that faced onto the street. Maybe Jennifer had decided to stand him up.

But there she was, finally, pausing just inside the door to look around. He raised a hand, and she caught the motion, nodded, and started toward him, weaving her way between the tables.

She wore black pants today, with a white knit tee topped by a bright pink sweater that seemed to make her olive skin glow. More than one of the college guys looked up as she went by, but she seemed unaware of their attention.

He rose as she reached him, pulling a chair out for her. "I was beginning to think you weren't coming."

"Sorry." The color in her cheeks deepened, and she flipped a menu open seemingly at random. "I had to speak to a parent of a new child in the preschool before I could get away."

"No problem. What do you feel like having for lunch?" Better to get the ordering over with so the hovering server would leave them alone before starting what was going to be a difficult conversation.

She glanced at the menu, then up at the server who waited, pen poised over his pad. "I guess I'll have the pecan chicken salad. And a chai latte, please."

The kid, probably a college student making a little spending money at the Half Joe, nodded, scribbling on the pad, and then looked at Mason.

"A reuben. And a refill on the coffee." He handed the menu over, relieved when the server walked away.

Except that he didn't know quite where to start. "Are your phones all set up now?"

She smiled, surprising him. "All set. I have to say that my dad was excited about the whole thing. It made him feel as if he's living in one of his favorite television shows."

"He's not upset about your involvement?" He'd expect her father to be outraged at the idea of his daughter getting mixed up in this mess.

"Not upset, exactly." She glanced up, smiling, as the server put a frothy brew in front of her, waiting until he moved away before continuing. "He's worried about my safety, I suppose. Well, I am, too." A shiver went through her. "Honestly, Mason, if you'd heard Penny—I don't think she's in her right mind."

"She can't be if it's true that she killed Josie to steal her baby." It took an effort to say the words evenly. Josie's baby. His baby?

"She all but admitted it to Kate."

He reached out to clasp her hand. Her eyes widened, but she didn't pull away. He had to get through to her.

"That's all the more reason why you shouldn't be involved. I'm sure your dad feels the same."

She was already shaking her head at that. "You don't know my dad very well if you think that. He's always been pretty high on doing your duty. Comes of being in the military for so long, I guess. He expects me to do the right thing, no matter how difficult."

"He's a unique person, then."

"You don't think that's what most fathers expect of their kids?"

He grimaced slightly. "I guess I'm not a very good judge. My father expected that I'd do what enhanced the Grant name. Or at least try not to sully it. He was usually disappointed."

"I'm sorry." Quick sympathy darkened her eyes. "It sounds as if you didn't get along very well with him."

"You could say that." They were straying from his goal into dangerous personal territory. He didn't want to make Jennifer feel sorry for him. He just wanted her to take his advice. "Look, about this business with Penny—"

She stiffened. "It's no use arguing about it, Mason. Besides, even if I wanted to get out of it, I couldn't. Penny's calling the shots right now."

"She doesn't have to." His fingers tightened on hers. "All you'd have to do is go away for a couple of days. Don't take your cell phone, and don't let anyone know where you're going. If she can't reach you, she'll have to call me."

"I can't." The smooth line of her jaw seemed to harden. "It's my problem. Not yours."

"I know how you feel." She moved her fingers along his hand comfortingly. "You want to take on all the responsibility. You were always that way."

Was he? Jennifer seemed to remember him differently than he remembered himself.

"But this time you can't." Her tone was final. "I'm not running away."

He should have known that would be her answer, but he had to try. "It *is* my responsibility. Not yours. If Josie's daughter is my child—"

He stopped, not wanting to explore that with Jennifer, of all people.

"If she is, what will you do then?" Her voice was soft, even though no one was close enough to hear. "What will you do if the tests prove that Alexis is your daughter?"

Jennifer's use of the child's name made her more real. And that didn't help.

"I don't know. I just don't know."

Jennifer looked at him steadily, and he could tell by the disappointed expression on her face that that was the wrong answer.

Three days had passed since her encounter with Penny Brighton, and Jennifer had finally stopped jumping every time the telephone rang. Dad, too, had gradually relaxed his vigilance, and he'd even agreed to go out to his weekly bowling match, promising he'd be home early.

She wasn't worried. Jennifer switched on the reading lamp beside her chair. It had grown dark while she'd been absorbed in the unit on Easter she was developing for the four-year-old class. A little light would help to banish the shadows that had gathered while she'd worked.

Well, Dad would be home soon. And it must be likely that Penny had been frightened off by all the police attention. She couldn't hope to elude the hunt for her much longer. She might already be hundreds of miles from Magnolia Falls.

Or Penny could have decided to contact Mason directly. He'd have told her, if so, wouldn't he?

She didn't have any illusions about why Penny had picked her as a go-between. She'd wanted someone she figured wouldn't fight back. It was rather demoralizing to know she'd assumed Jennifer was that person.

She didn't want to think about that. Think about Mason, instead.

But she wasn't sure that was any better. She'd been touched by Mason's obvious concern for her. He wanted to protect her.

Not that his attitude meant anything, she hastened to remind herself. Mason thought of her as a friend, that was all.

There had been those moments in the church gym—moments when it seemed things were about to change between them. But he'd backed away from that, and he hadn't shown by word or expression any sign that he wanted more than friendship from her.

She stared absently at the list of possible art activities she'd drawn up, unable to concentrate on them. She wasn't looking for a relationship, in any event. Until she was ready to trust another human being with her deepest secrets and failings, she wouldn't be ready for anything serious, and there were times when she thought that would be never.

The jangle of the telephone in the kitchen set her nerves jangling, too. Maybe she wasn't quite as over this as she'd been telling herself she was.

Quickly, before the machine could pick up, she hurried to the kitchen and reached for the wall phone. She put it gingerly to her ear, as if something ugly was about to come out of the receiver.

"Hello?"

No answer.

"Hello?" More emphatic. "Is someone there?"

"Actually no." The voice spoke from behind her. "I'm here."

She whirled. Penny stood in her kitchen, just inside the door. She seemed perfectly at ease, smiling a little, wearing faded jeans and a gray T-shirt. She held a cell phone in one hand. In the other, she carried a small gun.

"How did you get in here?" She'd locked the door after Dad left—she knew she had.

"You should get better locks," Penny said in that deceptively soft Southern drawl of hers. "A five-year-old could pop that one. Hang up the phone."

Jennifer shivered slightly as she obeyed. She folded

her arms so that Penny couldn't see her hands tremble. At least she'd pretend she wasn't frightened.

"What do you want?"

"Why, Jennifer, anyone would think you're not glad to see me."

"The last time we met, you threatened to push me into the swamp. I don't know why you'd think I should be happy to welcome you into my home." There, that was better. It didn't sound as frightened as she felt.

"You talked to Mason." Penny smiled. "You rushed right over to see him. To find out if it was true. Does he admit it?"

A chill crept down her spine. Had Penny followed her that night? Or was she guessing? It was the obvious thing for her to have done.

"Well, does he?" Penny's voice went up, and the hand holding the gun thrust toward her.

She recoiled. Penny might try to sound cool and in control, but she was teetering on the edge of reason at this very moment.

"Mason told me about his relationship with Josie." She shouldn't tell Penny that he'd already submitted to DNA testing. The trap depended on Penny believing that Mason would pay for her silence. "He knows I can keep a secret." That was as close as she could come to lying about it.

"Of course you can, especially when it comes to Mason Grant. You always did have a crush on him, but he never looked twice at you."

"We were friends." She couldn't help stiffening at the taunt. Penny was striking out blindly. She couldn't possibly know anything about Jennifer's feelings. "We still are."

"Good. As a friend, I'm sure you'll want to help him out of this predicament he's in. After all, he wouldn't want the police to know that he had a very good reason for killing Josie."

Did Penny really think that she wasn't the prime suspect? She was the one who had taken Josie's child, and she'd admitted her guilt to Kate.

The chill intensified. Penny looked like any normal woman, but she wasn't. There was something seriously skewed inside her—something that let her see other people as pawns to be moved around as she willed. Something that kept her from recognizing the results of her actions.

"Mason is willing to pay you." Jennifer forced her voice to sound calm. "Just tell me when and where you want him to take the money."

Quickly. Dad could come home at any moment.

Please, Lord. Don't let him walk in on this. He'd try to protect me, but what could he do against a gun?

"Are you eager to get this over with?" Penny arched an eyebrow. "Fine. Tomorrow night. Nine o'clock. The Nature Preserve."

The Nature Preserve. Her throat tightened. The preserve was a nice place to visit during the day, but its meandering paths through the woods, with swampy areas and lagoons where gators lurked were no place for anyone to be at night.

"How will he know how to find you? The preserve is a big place."

Penny took a step back, toward the kitchen door. "Don't worry. Just walk along the trail from the east gate. I'll find you."

It took a moment for the word to register. "Me?"

Penny smiled, as if pleased at her reaction. "You, Jennifer. You'll do that for your old friend, won't you?" Her tone was mocking. "You wouldn't let Mason down, now would you?"

"But—he won't let me. You must know he won't let me take his place in a situation like that."

"He'd better." Penny's voice went flat, and she lifted the gun until the black hole of the barrel was all that Jennifer could see. "You'll convince him. You'll be there with the money, or I'll have to pay you another visit." She smiled thinly. "You wouldn't want to end up like Josie, now would you?"

The police technical van was pulled up a few miles from the Nature Preserve, along with vehicles belonging to the detectives and to Jennifer. She slid out of the car, pulling her cardigan around her in the evening chill, very aware of Mason getting out of the passenger side.

She'd been surprised when the police agreed to Mason's presence tonight, even more surprised when he'd insisted on riding with her. In fact, he'd wanted to drive her in his car, but the detectives had pointed out that Penny would expect her to come in her own.

She glanced at Mason's face. He looked stern and withdrawn in the reflected gleam of the multiple head-lights. He hadn't said more than a few words during the

drive, leaving her uncertain why he'd been so determined to come along.

He looked at her now, his gaze searching. "Are you
all right?"

"Yes." She pulled her cardigan more tightly around
her. "A little scared, I guess." She smiled ruefully and
shook her head. "Make that a lot scared."

"You shouldn't be doing this—"

"Miss Pappas?" Nikki Rivers approached, her gaze
moving from Mason to Jennifer. "If you'll just step into
the van, we'll fix you up with a listening device. It'll let
us hear everything that you do."

"Will it get you to her in time if there's any trouble?"
Mason stepped forward, as if he'd keep her from getting
in the van.

"Just allow us do our job, Grant." Paterson moved
alongside Mason, nodding to the female detective to
proceed with Jennifer. "Come on over here and take a
look at the map of the preserve with me."

She climbed quickly into the van. Should she apolo-
gize for Mason's interference? But his actions weren't
her responsibility, and to imply that they were was to
claim a relationship that didn't exist.

Once she'd climbed into the van, Nikki Rivers
worked quickly, attaching the listening device under
Jennifer's sweater. Jennifer winced a little as it touched
her bare skin.

"Sorry." The woman hesitated a moment. "I'm afraid
it's cold. But necessary."

"I understand. Believe me, anything that makes me
feel safer is worth it."

Rivers cocked her head, apparently listening to the men's voices echoing from outside the van. "Mr. Grant is still objecting to your doing this. He's very concerned about your safety." There was almost, but not quite, a question in her tone.

"He'd feel that way about anyone taking a risk that he feels should be his."

"I can understand that." Rivers raised her eyebrows toward the technician, who fiddled with his earpiece and then gave her an okay sign. "Unfortunately, if we let him do this, chances are good the Brighton woman wouldn't show at all. She probably doesn't want to risk getting too close to him—afraid he might try to resolve this by tackling her."

"You have to catch her." Jennifer suppressed a shiver at the memory of Penny in her kitchen. Of the gun she'd held. "She all but admitted that she killed Josie and stole her baby."

"Unfortunately we need a little more than that to charge her with murder." Rivers snapped a switch on the device. "There, we'll leave it off for now. Just slide the button to the on position when you reach the parking lot. Okay?"

She nodded. They'd already gone over all of this before they left Magnolia Falls. She knew what was expected of her. She knew, as well, that there was no way the police could stay close behind her on that winding nature trail, not if they wanted to keep Penny from knowing they were there.

"But you'll arrest her. If she shows up tonight, you will arrest her, won't you?"

"Oh, yes." Rivers patted her shoulder. "We certainly

have enough to hold her on a variety of charges. It's just that a ten-year-old murder can be hard to pin down without a confession or solid evidence."

Jennifer nodded. It didn't really matter to her what they charged Penny with, so long as they put her away. And then that little girl—

"What's happening to the child? Alexis? Is it definite that she's Josie's?"

Rivers hesitated for a moment, and then she nodded. "The powers-that-be are still arguing over which of them should conduct a news conference, but I understand a public announcement will be made tomorrow, regardless of what happens tonight. DNA tests prove the child is hers, and I understand her sister is here from Florida to look after her for the moment."

"Until the father is identified, you mean."

Rivers shrugged, evading her eyes. "I guess."

And if that father proved to be Mason, what would he do? He didn't seem eager to jump into instant fatherhood, but still—

That little girl deserved parents who loved her. Every child deserved that. Penny had robbed her of her mother. She had to have someone.

Please, Lord. She closed her eyes briefly, her heart hurting in sympathy for that child, who must be confused and in pain. *Be with Alexis. Let her feel the comfort of Your love.*

"Ready?" The detective looked at her with raised eyebrows.

She nodded. Ready as she was likely to be. She stepped out of the van.

Mason was waiting. "Give us a moment, will you please?"

Rivers shrugged, moving off for a low-voiced conversation with her colleague.

Mason frowned down at her. "Is everything we say being recorded?"

"No. I'm not going to turn it on until I reach the parking lot."

Alone. She'd be alone then, in that gravel lot under the trees. She could imagine how dark it would be there in spite of the nearly full moon.

Mason took her hands, holding them between both of his. "You're cold." His tone was almost angry.

But he wasn't angry with her. She knew that. He was angry over the situation.

"Not really." She forced a smile. "That's just nerves, I think. My hands are always cold when I'm nervous."

They were warming now, caught in his firm grasp. In fact, it felt as if he were warming her heart, as well. The strength that flowed from him was almost enough to take the fear away.

"I hate it that you have to do this. You can still back out, you know."

"No." That much she knew. "I can't."

He rubbed her hands gently. "You're scared. You have to be."

She nodded. "Penny—well, Penny was enough to scare anyone."

"She threatened you." His voice roughened. "I'm sorry. Sorry that knowing me got you into this."

"It wasn't the threats. Or at least, that wasn't the

worst part. I mean, there she stood, looking so much like the girl she was in college. And yet when she talked, I felt as if she were teetering on the brink of—" She shivered a little. "I don't know what the definition of insanity is. But she certainly doesn't react like any normal person."

"All the more reason why you shouldn't confront her alone." Pain filled his voice suddenly.

"Don't, Mason." Impulsively she put her hand on his chest, feeling the steady beat of his heart against her palm. "I know you'd do anything to take my place, but you can't. And I..." Her voice gained strength. "I wouldn't choose this, but I don't think God would have put this challenge in front of me if He didn't intend to see me through."

Mason's hand enveloped hers, holding it close to his heart. "I hope you're right. I just wish there was something I could do."

"You can pray," she whispered.

He stiffened. She felt it through their linked hands. "I'm not the best person for that. God doesn't seem to listen to me anymore."

That jolted her down to her toes. She'd known there was something, but she hadn't imagined this. She wanted to talk to him, find out what was wrong in his faith life, but this wasn't the moment for that.

"Pray anyway," she said. "Promise me."

He nodded, his mouth twisting a little. "I promise."

Gravel crunched under Rivers's shoe as she approached. "Are you ready, Miss Pappas?"

Jennifer breathed a silent prayer. "Yes. I'm ready."

SEVEN

Jennifer pulled into the gravel parking lot at the nature preserve, her fingers tight on the steering wheel. Darkness pressed against the car windows, so tangible she imagined a weight on the glass.

Dear Father, I'm afraid. Please, be with me now. Give me the courage to do what has to be done.

She pulled up to the opening to the trail, letting her headlamps shine into the dark tunnel it made in the forest. Nothing. She couldn't see anyone. Not that she'd expected to. Penny wouldn't be standing there waiting for her.

Penny would be cautious, Jennifer reasoned. Penny's malice might be frightening, but it wasn't mindless. She had definite aims, and she'd do whatever she could to minimize the risk to herself. Naturally, she'd hang back, wanting to be sure Jennifer hadn't been followed by the police before she showed herself.

If Penny knew Jennifer was involved in trying to trap her… A shudder went through her. She didn't want to imagine what Penny would do if she realized that. Certainly Penny was ruthless. Anyone who'd kill a friend in order to steal her baby…

Well, that hadn't been proven yet, but what else could have happened? If Penny had some logical explanation for how she'd ended up with Josie's child, surely she'd have explained herself long ago.

She couldn't sit here, letting herself get more frightened by the moment. She had to move.

She switched on the tiny microphone Nikki Rivers had taped to her skin under her shirt, and then adjusted the earpiece. It crackled to life instantly.

"Miss Pappas? What's happening?" Rivers's voice spoke in her ear, so close it was as if she sat behind her.

Just speak naturally, they'd told her. *The microphone will pick it up.*

"I'm fine." She thought of Mason. He'd be in the truck with the detectives, listening to her voice. She didn't want to sound like a wimp in front of him. "I'm parked in the lot. There's no sign of anyone else here."

"She may be waiting for you somewhere along the trail," Rivers pointed out. "Just remember not to say anything once you're out of the car until you meet her. You don't want to tip her off that you're wired."

"I know." They didn't have to remind her to be careful where Penny was concerned. She wasn't likely to forget.

"I'm getting out now." She grasped the handle of the case that lay next to her on the passenger seat, a shiver going down her spine.

Money—a lot of money. Probably more than she'd ever seen in cash before.

The police had suggested loading the case with cut

paper, but Mason had gone ballistic at that. What if something went wrong and Penny opened the case before the police reached them? Penny might take it out on Jennifer. He'd insisted that she carry the real thing, and he'd provided the money.

She hated the idea of being responsible for that much cash, but his attitude had warmed her.

She slammed the car door, shutting off the comforting glow of the dome light, and switched on the heavy flashlight she carried. Not even Penny could expect her to wander down that trail through the woods without a light. Breathing another prayer, she started down the winding path.

The parking lot disappeared from view almost immediately when the path curved, seeming to close her in with the dense growth of pine and live oaks.

She was afraid, but God was with her.

If only she could speak, could be connected to those waiting a mile away in the police van, even if just by voice, it would not be as frightening. But she couldn't. She had to play her part if this were to have any chance of success.

It would be worth any amount of fear if the police caught Penny and resolved this once and for all. Then they could all stop living in the shadow of suspicion.

The flashlight beam caught a pair of eyes, glowing red in the reflected light, and her heart thumped in her chest. A possum turned, waddling slowly out of sight, and she could breathe again.

Did the silent listeners detect her fear? She hoped not. If they did—well, they could hardly blame her. She'd been to the nature preserve several times during the day, but alone, at night—that was a different story.

She had been here once at night. Not on the forest trail, but at the picnic grove on the far side of the parking lot, overlooking the small lake. Early May, their senior year. It had been the last Campus Christian Fellowship event of the semester, and the final time for their little group of seniors to be together.

She seemed to see the laughing faces reflected in the glow of the campfire. Kate, with her beautiful voice, had led the singing, moving easily from one favorite gospel song to another.

Jennifer's heart seemed to clench. They'd been so young then, so untried by life. Ten years made a huge difference. After college one had to sink or swim out in the big wide world. They'd been on the cusp of that, teetering between eagerness to get on with their lives and fear at leaving the familiar cocoon of college behind them.

Maybe it wasn't so accurate to say they'd been untried by life, though. Certainly Josie had been. She must have known by then that she was pregnant. What had she been thinking? Had she been afraid? Longing to tell someone her secret?

Mason had come before the evening was over, surprising all of them. He hadn't been around much that semester after his father died. Too busy trying to manage the family business and complete his coursework so that he could graduate with his class. But he'd come that night—arriving late and leaving early, as she recalled.

She had no trouble remembering how the firelight

had flickered on the strong planes of his face, cast shadows around his eyes. They'd been happy to see him, with everyone in a mood to reminisce, but he'd been quiet and withdrawn.

Because Josie was there? She tried to look at that evening through the lens of what she knew now. Had he and Josie spoken? Impossible to remember that, even if she'd noticed at the time. And whether they did or didn't, it wouldn't prove anything.

Only the cold science of DNA testing would reveal the truth about the identity of Alexis's father.

She did remember one thing, though, the image as clear in her mind as if it had happened yesterday. She'd seen Mason walking toward his car and, on impulse, she'd run after him.

"You're not going already?" She'd caught up with him at the edge of the parking lot. "We haven't even made the smores yet."

His eyebrows had lifted. "Tempting me with chocolate, Jennifer? I'm sorry, but I have to get going."

"I'm sorry, too. For everything." She had reached out, touching the sleeve of his shirt lightly, longing to say something that would chase that somber look from his eyes.

"What do you mean?" He looked startled, but then his eyes narrowed.

"Why, about your father. What else? I haven't had a chance to talk to you alone since it happened."

"That." He shrugged. "Thanks. I'm doing okay. I just have a lot on my plate with running the stores and looking after my mother."

"I wish there was something I—we—could do. All your friends are concerned about you," she added quickly.

He'd given her a look she'd found impossible to interpret. Had he wanted to speak then? If so, he'd changed his mind. He'd shaken his head, a lock of blond hair tumbling onto his forehead.

"Sweet Jennifer. You always want to fix everything for your friends." His face seemed to tighten. "Some things can't be fixed."

He'd turned and walked toward his car, and in a moment he'd pulled out of the lot and basically out of her life for ten years.

Until the reunion had brought them all back together again, for good or ill.

A splash somewhere off to her right jerked her attention back to the present, her pulse quickening. A splash meant she'd already reached the lagoon.

She shivered. Alligators. Water snakes. She'd seen both from a safe distance when she'd wandered along the trail during the day. She had no wish to encounter them at night. Alone. Penny would almost be preferable.

She swung the light around, catching a glimpse of water through the thick growth of trees. She was almost at the end of the trail. Where was Penny? Was this all her idea of a sick joke?

Another sound, louder now, as a branch snapped and something rustled in the undergrowth. She froze, gasping, her heart pounding so loudly she could hear it.

Rivers's voice sounded instantly in her ear. "What is it? Is something wrong? Do you see her? If you do, say something."

Jennifer's nails bit into her palms. If she spoke to them and Penny lurked in the bushes, she'd know it was a trap.

"Penny?" she called out, her voice wavering a little. "Penny, is that you? Come out where I can see you."

Surely that sounded natural enough, and at least it alerted the police. And Mason, waiting with them.

Another sound in the bushes. Fear clutched her throat. "Penny?" She tried to ignore the chatter in her ear and focus on the sound. "Where are—"

A dark shape hurtled out of the bushes toward her. She stumbled back a step, letting out a cry, losing the torch as she hit the ground.

In the instant Mason heard Jennifer's cry, the breath went out of him. Someone shoved him out of the way as police erupted out of the tech van. He stumbled, then jumped out after them. Jennifer was in trouble. He had to get to her.

"Wait here." Paterson flung the order over his shoulder as he and Rivers jumped into a waiting car. Ignoring him, Mason yanked the back door open and fell inside as the cop accelerated.

"What—"

"Never mind," Rivers said. "Just get there."

Cars pulled out, sirens wailing as they flew down the narrow blacktop road toward the preserve. Just a mile, that's all. Just a mile and they'd be there.

Please. The word formed in his mind. *I know I don't deserve anything from You. But Jennifer is innocent. Protect her. Be with her now.*

He'd given up praying a long time ago. Maybe it was a measure of how much Jennifer had come to mean to him that he did it now.

The cars shrieked into the parking lot at the far end of the nature trail. Jennifer couldn't have been more than a hundred yards from the end of the trail when whoever, whatever interrupted her. They'd be there soon.

Please. Please.

The car stopped in a spray of gravel, and he was out even before the cops. But Paterson grabbed him before he could dart toward the shadowy opening to the trail.

"Wait here," the man snarled. Taking obedience for granted, he joined the officers already racing toward the trail.

The instant their lights rounded the first curve in the path, Mason went after them. Jennifer was out there, alone and in danger, because of him. He couldn't stay behind.

Brambles grabbed at his legs as he ran, and the eerie shapes of live oaks draped with Spanish moss seemed to converge over his head. How could he have let Jennifer come out here alone? If something had happened to her, it would be his fault.

He burst around the last twist in the path into a confused scene—flashes of bright torches, dark figures—and Jennifer, sitting on the ground, her back against the straight trunk of a pine. Nikki Rivers bent over her.

He took a frantic step or two toward her before he forced himself to stop.

She was alive. She seemed to be alert and talking.

He didn't have the right to involve her in the mess

he'd made of his life. Holding his emotions on a tight rein, he went close enough to hear her voice.

"I'm all right. Really. I just got the wind knocked out of me."

Rivers, seeming unconvinced, ran her hand over the back of Jennifer's head. "Sure you didn't hit your head when you fell?"

"I'm fine," Jennifer repeated. Her face was pale in the gleam of the flashlights, but her jaw was set. It wouldn't do to let her know how much his heart was wrung by the brave front she put on.

"I'm sorry." She shook her head. "I shouldn't have panicked."

"The Brighton woman?" Paterson said urgently. "Did you see her? Where did she go?"

Jennifer shook her head. "It wasn't her. It was a deer. I must have startled it, and when I tried to get out of the way, it darted in the same direction." She rubbed her shoulder, wincing a little. "It hit my shoulder, knocking me to the ground. There was no sign of Penny the whole time."

Paterson muttered something under his breath, swinging his light in a wide circle, as if hoping to catch Penny lingering in the undergrowth.

"Forget it," Rivers advised. "She's long gone now. If she was ever here."

"If she was here, she knows now it was a trap. She won't try the same thing again." Paterson sounded disgusted.

"I'm sorry—" Jennifer began.

"It's not your fault," Mason said quickly. "You did your part."

The look she turned on him was so full of gratitude that it pierced his heart. She had no business being grateful to him. He was the one who owed her.

"What about the money?" Rivers asked. "You didn't drop it in the swamp, did you?"

"No." Jennifer pulled the case from behind her and thrust it toward Mason. "You take it. I don't want to be responsible for it any longer."

He took the case, feeling as if she were pushing him away along with the money. He wanted to say something to make this better for her. To let her know how sorry he was and find out what was going on with her.

But he couldn't. He didn't have the right to force himself that deeply into her heart and soul.

An image flashed into his mind. Maybe it had been lurking there since he'd known they were coming to the nature preserve tonight.

Senior year. The last get-together of CCF for the graduating seniors.

He could see the campfire burning in the background, and the glitter of moonlight reflecting on the calm water of the lake.

They'd all been sitting around the fire, reminiscing, and he hadn't been able to sit there any longer, seeing Josie across from him, wanting to make things right with her and unable to.

He'd walked away, finally, but someone had come after him. Jennifer. She'd stopped him in the parking lot, the sound of singing voices drifting to them on the evening breeze.

She'd offered him her caring, her sympathy, holding it out as a gift of her generous heart. And he'd been so upset with himself over Josie that he'd rejected it.

She'd probably thought that he was rejecting her friendship, as well.

It was too late. He couldn't mend things with Jennifer now, just as he hadn't been able to do it then.

EIGHT

From the top of a nearby hill, parked deep in the shadow of a country church, Penny watched. And fumed, nails tapping against the steering wheel as she followed the lights bobbing in the woods.

They were stupid to think she wouldn't take precautions. She'd checked out this area long before she'd chosen the nature preserve as the meeting place, wanting to be sure there was a safe vantage point.

Which this was. From here, she'd seen Jennifer's car pull into the lot, seen the solitary figure start down the trail. She waited to be sure no one followed, catching sight of nothing but the single light flickering through the trees.

When she was sure, she'd driven down the hill, approaching the lot at the end of the trail. The plan was to wait there until Jennifer emerged, grab the money and be gone before she could get back to her own car.

It hadn't worked out that way. She'd rolled down the window, listening intently for any sound that would tell her where Jennifer was, and she'd been rewarded for her patience.

She'd heard a faint cry, and she'd gritted her teeth in annoyance because Jennifer had been stupid enough to get herself into trouble on the trail. She'd almost gotten out of the car. Then, with her hand on the door handle, she'd heard something else, something that forced her heart into high gear. The wail of sirens, coming fast.

She'd peeled out of there and been back in her shelter by the time the cop cars pulled into the lot. She watched, impotent, as the beams of their powerful torches darted through the woods.

She gripped the wheel until her fingers hurt. A trap. Stupid little Jennifer had called in the police, had dared to set a trap for her. Mason, too. She wouldn't have done it without his connivance.

She forced herself to take a couple of deep breaths. She couldn't let the anger take over. Use it, but don't let it rule her.

All right, so she'd thought she'd had wimpy do-gooder Jennifer pegged, and she'd been surprised. She couldn't allow the thirst for revenge to distract her from the important thing. The money.

Think. The police were here, so that had to mean that Mason had admitted his relationship with Josie. Blackmailing him over that secret was off the table.

Still, what about the kid? It would be too hard to snatch Alexis from that boarding school—Penny's parents had long ago alerted the faculty to not let her anywhere near Alexis. Besides, the police would likely have the school grounds under watch.

But once Mason was established as the father, Alexis would come to Magnolia Falls. So what if Mason hadn't been willing to pay to keep secret his fatherhood of Alexis? That made it all the more likely that he'd pay to keep her safe.

She smiled in satisfaction at the plan that was growing in her mind. She could stay in hiding for a little longer, uncomfortable as it was. Long enough to put Mason in a position where he'd be happy to give her the money in exchange for his daughter's safety.

And as for Jennifer—rage coursed through her veins. She had a score to settle with her. Jennifer would learn that she always paid her scores in full.

She started the car, headlights off to avoid attracting attention, and drove away.

Jennifer slid the bin of preschool toys into the cabinet and closed the doors, glancing around the classroom to be sure it was ready for the onslaught of after-school kids.

Two days. It had been two full days since that fiasco at the nature preserve, and she hadn't heard a word from Mason.

Maybe that was for the best. Their past had been buried for ten years, like poor Josie. They couldn't bring it back.

She couldn't help but feel that she hadn't been at her best the other night, scared to death by a deer. Still, one good thing had come out of it. The police were convinced that since Penny hadn't shown up, she must have lost her nerve and run off.

She could be at the Mexican border by now, Paterson had pointed out. They'd undoubtedly seen the last of her.

Jennifer wasn't entirely sure she agreed with the detective's analysis. She didn't buy the idea that Penny would have lost her nerve. But Penny might have decided that trying to blackmail Mason was too dangerous.

Actually, she didn't care why Penny had left the area, only that she was far, far away from Magnolia Falls by now, and out of their lives.

She glanced toward the doorway at the sound of footfalls in the hall. Couldn't be the kids—they made far more noise than that.

Mason paused in the doorway, and one look at him told her that something was wrong.

"Hi." She moved toward him tentatively. She hadn't seen that expression in his face before. He looked—stunned. "What's going on?"

Something seemed to move in his eyes, as if it took an effort for him to focus on her. He swallowed, and she saw the convulsive movement of his neck.

"I got the results back from the DNA test. I am the father of Josie's child."

She'd thought she'd accepted it. She discovered she hadn't. That faint trace of jealousy—where had it come from?

Forgive me, Lord. And show me how to help Mason, as well as the child.

"How do you feel about it?" She made an effort to keep her voice neutral.

He shook his head. "Dazed, I guess. I never intended…" He stopped short.

A tiny pang pierced her heart. "I don't suppose Josie did, either."

He rubbed his temples, as if his head hurt. "I meant, I never intended to be a father at all."

Final Justice

She could only stare at him. "Mason, but surely—"

"That's not important now. The question is, what am I going to do about the child?"

"Alexis," she said firmly. "She has a name."

He gave her a startled look. "Alexis," he repeated. "I'm sorry. She doesn't seem quite real to me."

She could understand, but he had to face this. "She is real. She's a little girl who's had everything she knows about herself turned upside down. She's going to need a lot of reassurance."

"That's just it." His hands moved, as if to push the situation away from him. "She needs more help than I can provide. I don't know a thing about kids, especially little girls."

Blowing up at him wouldn't help the situation any, tempting as it was.

Please, Lord. Give me patience. She took a step back, bumping into the child-size table. *Help me to help him see how much this little girl needs him.*

"Maybe not," she said gently. "But Alexis needs her father."

"Father." His mouth twisted on the word. "What do I know about being a father?"

The bitterness in his voice startled her. She had to tread carefully. She reached out to touch his hand with her fingertips. "What is it, Mason? Your father—"

He shook his head, jaw tense. "My family could have been the poster family for dysfunctional."

She wrapped her fingers around his, seeming to feel the pain that he was trying so hard to suppress. "Tell me about it."

His hand turned, and he twined his fingers with hers. "You never met any of them, did you?"

She shook her head. "I know you had a brother who died."

"Gerry." His mouth softened. "He was six years older than I was. The greatest big brother in the world."

"Not so dysfunctional then."

"Not between me and Gerry. But our parents—" He shrugged. "They made it clear all my life that Gerry was the son they'd wanted. I was just an accident."

"Surely they didn't feel that." Her mind jumped to her own big, loving family. With four boys younger than her, the house had sometimes been chaotic, but Mom and Dad had managed to find time to make each of their kids feel special.

"Didn't they?" He gave her a look that suggested she had no idea. "If I'd ever had any doubts, they vanished when Gerry died. Do you know what my father said to me when we stood in the church, facing each other over my brother's coffin? He said the wrong son had died." His mouth twisted. "He could afford to lose me. Not Gerry."

Her heart was wrenched with his pain. "Oh, my dear." She reached up instinctively to touch his face, wanting to ease the lines of pain away. "Don't. Don't let it hurt so much. If they didn't appreciate the person you are, it was their loss."

He put his hand over hers, pressing her palm against his cheek. She felt the warmth of his skin, the slight stubble of his beard, and it sent a tingle radiating along her flesh.

"They were right." His voice had thickened, as if his

throat was tight. "Gerry was the golden boy. Smart, kind, a great athlete, popular. He was a son to be proud of."

"You loved him." She leaned toward him, longing to wipe the pain from his face. "But that doesn't mean they were right. Don't you see that?"

His eyes focused on hers, and they darkened. Her skin seemed to warm, and she felt as if the breath had gone out of her. She swayed toward him.

"Jennifer." His voice was soft. He slid his hands up her arms, grasping her shoulders and drawing her closer.

She should say something. She couldn't. She leaned toward him, caught in a tide that was too strong for her. When his lips claimed hers, it was inevitable.

Mason's hands were strong and warm on her shoulders. Other than that, only their lips touched, but she felt as if they were linked in a way she'd only been able to imagine before.

Her heart swelled. She cared for him. She'd always cared for him. But—

He drew back, and she saw written on his face the same confusion she felt.

"Sorry." He managed a rueful smile. "Guess that was bad timing."

"I guess so." She wanted to deny it, to say that she was ready for whatever a relationship with him would bring, but she couldn't.

She couldn't get involved with anyone without telling him about her past, and even though instinct assured her that Mason could be trusted, she couldn't burden him with that now. Not when he had so much else to deal with.

She took a step back, resting her hand on the children's table. Oddly enough, that seemed to stabilize her. The child was important now, far more important than her feelings.

He shook his head, as if to clear it. "I didn't come here to do that. I'm sorry. I wanted to talk to you about Alexis. To figure out the best thing to do."

"Is there really any question?" She locked her emotions away to consider later. "Alexis is your daughter. You're all that she has left now. You have to take care of her."

He raised an eyebrow. "Even if I make as lousy a parent as my dad?"

"You could hardly be a worse parent than Penny, could you?"

"You have a point there." He ran his fingers through his hair. "I guess the truth is that I'm scared."

"I can understand that." She wanted to reach toward him, but it was probably best not to touch him again. "Still, it seems to me that the best thing you can do is give that little girl stability and certainty right now. The rest will come in time."

He took a deep breath. "You're right about one thing. I may not know anything about being a good father, but I'm all she's got." He focused on her. "You, on the other hand, are an expert where kids are concerned. Will you help me, Jennifer?"

A hand seemed to squeeze her hand. Helping him with Alexis would mean getting closer to him. Getting closer to heartache.

But when could she ever turn down a child in need? She tried to smile.

"Of course I'll help. I'll do anything you need."

No matter what the cost.

He was about to meet the daughter he'd never known existed. He sat alone on a park bench, watching the spring sunshine filter through veils of Spanish moss and trying to make sense of the changes that had turned his life upside down.

Across the park, a father pushed his child on the rustic swing set. The little girl—four or five, maybe— laughed, her light voice floating to him on the sultry air.

"Higher, Daddy. Higher."

A cold hand seemed to squeeze his heart. What did he know about being a father? His own father certainly hadn't set much of an example. If his father were alive today, he'd be quick to point out that this was just another opportunity for Mason to fail someone.

He couldn't fail this child. She didn't deserve that after all she'd been through. But he was probably the last person in the world who should be trusted with the responsibility for her.

He glanced at his watch. They would come soon, and his life would change irrevocably. To his relief, he saw Jennifer walking toward him on the path. Somehow the fact that she'd be with him made this seem easier.

Maybe it was best that he didn't look at that fact too closely. He rose when she came closer.

"Thanks." He suppressed the urge to take her hand. "I'm glad you're here."

Jennifer's brow furrowed. "I hope this is the right

thing to do. I wouldn't want Alexis to get the wrong idea about our relationship."

"She won't. She'll just think I'm lucky to have such a good friend."

That didn't remove the worry from Jennifer's face, but she didn't pursue the matter.

Was he taking advantage of her? That thought had occurred to him too often to be dismissed.

Still, Jennifer was by way of being an expert on children, and he certainly needed an expert right now.

"I ought to fill you in on what I've learned from Shelley, Josie's sister." Concentrate on facts, and leave the emotion out of the equation. That was the only way to get through this.

Jennifer nodded. "Please."

He took a breath, marshalling his thoughts. "According to Shelley, Penny wasn't what you call an exemplary mother. She moved around a lot, and apparently dumped Alexis on anyone who'd take her."

Jennifer made a small, distressed sound. "Poor child."

He nodded. "Fortunately Penny's parents stepped in. As far as Shelley could find out, they were the most stable influence in Alexis's life for several years."

"But she's not with them now?"

"They're fairly elderly, and they started to develop some serious health problems. It sounds as if they didn't want to let Penny take over, even if she would have. So they enrolled Alexis in a boarding school in Charleston." He didn't have any trouble interpreting Jennifer's look of distress at that. "I know that doesn't sound appropriate at her age, but that seems to have been the only option. And the school has an excellent reputation—they have lots of girls whose parents are in the mission field or abroad on diplomatic service."

"Still, a child that age needs a home."

"The grandparents aren't far away, and they've been seeing her frequently." He paused. "Except I guess they aren't the grandparents really, are they?"

"They are to Alexis," Jennifer said quickly. "You have to let her know that she can see them often. That is— I suppose they want to, don't they? Do you know how they've been taking all this?"

"Devastated, according to Detective Rivers, who talked to them. But they want to maintain their relationship with Alexis."

Jennifer nodded, her worried look easing. "Reassure her about that right away. It's probably been the biggest thing on her mind. Has she talked about it at all?"

She was sounding like the professional he knew her to be, and he found that comforting. Apparently he needed reassurance, just as Alexis did.

Small wonder he'd given in to the longing to kiss Jennifer yesterday. Or that he'd been thinking about it ever since.

He'd drawn back, because turning to Jennifer for comfort had reminded him too forcefully of that night with Josie, when he'd turned to her for comfort and precipitated all this. Would Josie still be alive if she hadn't gotten pregnant that night?

"According to Shelley, she hasn't talked about much of anything." Worry drew in around him. "You're the expert. How much is a child likely to be damaged by something like this?"

"I'm a teacher, not a child psychologist. Alexis may need more help than I can give." Jennifer stared down at her hands, clasped tightly in her lap. "Does anyone have any idea what was behind all of it? Why did Penny take Josie's baby to begin with?"

He shrugged. "No one is telling me much. But the police did say that Penny apparently tried to convince the Kessler family that the baby was hers and Adam's. They didn't believe it, because she wouldn't agree to a blood test."

"Steff mentioned something about that." She shivered, as it the thought chilled her. "What kind of person is she if she'd steal her friend's baby for the sake of inheriting a share of the Kessler fortune?"

"Not a very stable one, that's for sure. Alexis is better off away from her, but—"

"You're not having doubts again, are you?" Jennifer's dark gaze fastened on his face.

He shrugged. "Just wondering what Alexis is going to think of me, I guess." He glanced across the park and stiffened. "I'll know soon. Here they come."

Shelley Skerritt Johnson was tall and slim, with the same long, straight brown hair as Josie. There the similarity ended, though. Josie had been shy—needy, somehow, as if she were always looking for someone to rescue her. Shelley had a confident tilt to her head and a sure stride that seemed to indicate she could handle what came her way.

As for the child—his heart seemed to stop at the first

glimpse of his daughter. Alexis had Josie's heart-shaped face, the same straight brows and dark brown hair. And the expression—that reminded him of Josie, too.

Small wonder that Kate had recognized the photo as that of Josie's child. Alexis wore pink pants and a matching pink plaid shirt that would have looked cheerful had it not been for the lost look on her face.

That look punched a hole in his heart. No child should have to look like that. A kid had a right to be happy. Alexis looked as if she'd been disappointed so many times that she'd stopped expecting anything to turn out all right.

And now she was stuck with him as a father. He seemed to hear his father's voice in the back of his mind.

You'll let her down. Just as you always let everyone down. That's what you do.

NINE

Jennifer swung her legs, pumping the swing. She'd feel like a kid again if it were not for the silent figure swinging listlessly next to her.

She stopped pumping, letting the pendulum movement slow.

She'd persuaded Alexis to go on the swings with her, giving Mason a chance to talk privately with Josie's sister. That had to be difficult, although to judge from their body language, Shelley didn't seem to be blaming Mason for what had happened.

Of course, Mason was already doing a fine job of blaming himself.

What were they talking about so intently? Alexis must be wondering with even more painful interest than hers. She glanced at the small, sweet face. She wasn't sure she'd even seen a child look so guarded. It wasn't going to be easy to get through to her.

As her father, Mason was the logical person to have custody of Alexis. Did Shelley agree, or did she intend to put up a fight for her?

Please, Lord, let the adults handle this in the best possible way for Alexis's well-being. It will be difficult enough for her to adjust without having them at odds.

She dragged her feet on the pine-needle mulch under the swing, coming to a halt next to Alexis. Every conversational effort had been met with a curt yes or no, but maybe she should try again. At least she might distract Alexis from what was happening between her aunt and her father.

"There's a nice tennis court at the other end of this park. Do you like to play tennis?"

Alexis shook her head, a wing of brown hair swinging down to shield her face. "I took lessons once. I didn't like it much. My grammie said..." She stopped, her fingers tight on the swing's rope.

Jennifer's heart twisted. The poor child probably wondered if she even had a grandmother now. How much damage could it do at her age to have all your primary relationships turned upside down?

She longed to say something reassuring, but how could she, when she didn't know for sure herself what the situation was going to be with the grandparents?

"I was never very good with sports like tennis." She tried to keep her tone casual. "I took dance lessons all through school, and I loved that. And I played basketball for a while, but I wasn't very coordinated with the ball."

Alexis darted a look at her. "We played basketball in gym class this year."

"Did you like it?"

Alexis shrugged, her face seeming to close again. "It was okay."

Well, she'd gotten a couple of sentences out of her, at least, even if it had been an uphill battle.

They dangled on the swings in silence. Alexis traced a circle in the pine needles with the toe of her sneaker. Suddenly her fingers twisted on the rope. "Did you know my real mother?"

Jennifer's throat tightened, and she had to clear it before she could speak. So that was what was in Alexis's mind.

"I knew her pretty well, back when we were in college." Think. What could she say that would help? "You look a lot like her, did you know that?"

She nodded. "Aunt Shelley showed me a picture." She fell silent again.

"It must seem funny to meet an aunt you never knew you had."

Alexis didn't respond.

"Did you ask her about your mother?"

For a moment she thought the child wouldn't answer that, either, but then Alexis nodded. "But she looked like she was going to cry. So I didn't ask any more."

Jennifer had to suppress the tears that prickled her eyes at the words. "I'll make a deal with you. You can ask me anything you want. I'll try to answer. And I promise not to cry. Okay?"

No response. The toe of the blue sneaker traced another complete circle. "Okay," she said softly.

Something that had been tense in Jennifer seemed to relax. If Alexis could trust her, maybe they could begin to build a relationship. Maybe she could break through that wall Alexis seemed to have erected around her feelings and find a way to help her.

And if she did get that close to Alexis, how much would that entangle her with Mason? She glanced up, trying to distract herself from that question, and saw Mason gesturing to her.

She slid off the swing. "It looks as if your dad and your aunt want us."

Alexis nodded, following suit. Her small face was studiously blank. What was she steeling herself against? Poor kid. All the surprises in her life had been bad ones recently.

They walked across the playground to where Mason and Shelley waited. She longed to put her hand on the child's shoulder, but held back. Something about Alexis's armor said that such a gesture wouldn't be welcome.

Alexis's steps slowed as they approached the two people waiting for them. *She's afraid of what they're going to say.* Jennifer had a moment of sudden insight. *Whatever it is will change her life yet again.*

Shelley drew Alexis close to her, her face concerned. "Your father and I have been talking, and we think the best thing would be for you to stay here with him. You can go to school here in Magnolia Falls for the rest of the term, and that way you can get to know each other. Is that okay with you?"

Alexis shrugged, staring down at her feet. "I guess it is."

Jennifer managed an unobtrusive glance at Mason. He schooled his emotions even better than his daughter did, but he'd had years more practice. Helping those two break through their own emotional barriers was going to be difficult.

That's what You want for me in this situation, isn't it, Father? Apprehension came with the insight. *I don't know if I can.* Her mind fled to the disastrous mistake she'd made with a child in the past. *Maybe I'm not the right person for the job.*

But the certainty grew deeper. That's why she'd been put in this place right now. God had a task for her. She could only hope He intended to give her the wisdom she needed to deal with it.

Shelley looked relieved that Alexis wasn't putting up objections to their plans. But that would be more natural for a ten-year-old, wouldn't it? The very fact that she passively allowed others to rearrange her life was troubling.

"We'll go back to Charleston and pack up your things," Shelley said briskly. "Get your school records, all that sort of thing. We can come back and move you in on Friday if that works?" She sent an inquiring look at Mason, who nodded.

"Friday it is." His voice didn't sound natural. He cleared his throat and tried again. "I'm glad you're coming to stay with me, Alexis."

Better, she thought. She caught his eye and mouthed the word grandparents, and he nodded.

"Maybe we could go back up to Charleston on Sunday afternoon and visit your *grandparents* if they're well enough. Would you like that?"

Something flickered in Alexis's brown eyes, and she nodded.

"Good. We'll do that, then." Mason still sounded a little forced, but at least he was trying.

It wouldn't be easy, she thought as they watched Shelley and Alexis walk back toward Shelley's car. But at least they'd made a start.

Once the car pulled out, Mason's gaze met hers. "It's worse than I thought. Shelley says she's been withdrawn like that since the first time she saw her. If she couldn't get through to her, how can I?"

"With patience. Understanding." She couldn't let him back out now, even though she understood his doubts. "Put yourself in her place. Everything she thought she knew about herself has been turned upside down. It doesn't sound as if her life with Penny was very good, but it was what she was used to. Now she's not even Alexis Kessler anymore, and the people she's been told were her parents all her life aren't. Wouldn't you be withdrawn in that situation?"

"I suppose so. But that doesn't mean I have a clue about how to handle it. What if I fail her?"

"You won't." She touched his hand. "I think you're going to have to trust in God's guidance."

Bleakness touched his features with frost. "I'm afraid I'm not very good at that anymore."

Her heart twisted at the despair in his words. This wasn't just about Alexis's future. It was about restoring Mason's faith in God, and she was afraid that job was too big for her.

"Are you sure this is necessary?" Mason paused with a paint roller in his hand, reluctant to put the first stroke on the wall.

Jennifer tied a red bandana over black hair that was

pulled back in a thick braid. She'd turned up on his doorstep early on Saturday morning, laden down with paint cans.

"Do you want Alexis to feel at home here or not? Her bedroom is very important to a ten-year-old girl. You don't want her to feel as if she's being shuffled into a guest room like a casual visitor."

"But how do you know she'll like this? Maybe she hates yellow."

Jennifer lifted her roller and put a decided swath of color on the wall. She nodded with satisfaction. "I know because I called her housemother at boarding school to find out what she liked and how she had her room decorated." She turned back to the wall.

Obvious. At least it had been to Jennifer, if not to him.

"I didn't even consider that."

She shrugged. "It's probably something a woman is more likely to see than a man." Her smile flickered. "I was into ballet at that age. I had posters of ballerinas on every wall and a lamp in the shape of ballet shoes. I still have the lamp, packed away just in case I have a daughter who likes ballet."

She was trying to excuse him, but he couldn't so easily excuse himself. "What did the housemother say that Alexis likes?"

"She's into sports, especially soccer and horseback riding. And she loves dogs, especially golden retrievers, although she didn't have a pet from what I could find out. Oh, and patchwork. She had a patchwork quilt and patchwork pillows in her room."

He started painting. All right, so he didn't know

much about decor for little girls' rooms, but soccer and horseback riding—that he could handle.

"Spring soccer is starting up now—someone came by the store to ask for donations. I could see if she wants to sign up for that."

"Good idea." Jennifer's look of approval warmed him. Encouraged him, making him feel as if he was on the right track.

"We could go horseback riding, I guess. I haven't been on a horse in years."

"She's not going to be judging you on your equestrian skills," Jennifer said. "Relax. Just be yourself."

"That's easy for you to say. Of course she'd like you. You know what to say to kids."

"I have four younger brothers, remember?"

"I'd forgotten. Guess that does make you an expert. Is that why you went into teaching?"

She tilted her head, considering. "I guess that had something to do about it. My mom had MS, so I helped out a lot with the boys."

"That must have been hard."

"Hard?" She seemed startled. "No, not at all. We're family. We all pulled together."

He tried to imagine his own family dealing with adversity that way. Impossible. "But you must have missed out on a lot."

She stopped what she was doing, turning toward him. There was a streak of yellow paint on her cheek, and several strands of dark hair had escaped the red bandana. His fingers tingled with the urge to brush them back away from the smooth skin of her cheek.

"I suppose there were things I didn't do because of my family situation, but I never thought of it as missing out on anything. We had fun together. We loved each other."

She obviously assumed that was the way a family was. There was no hint in her voice that she considered her family unique. Maybe that explained why she thought he could create a home for Alexis.

Maybe. At least he could paint a wall if he couldn't do anything else.

"So you got your teaching degree from Magnolia College, but you didn't stay around here afterward?"

"Dad was transferred to upstate New York, so I looked for a job there. I wanted to be close enough to see them often. Then after my mom died, when my dad wanted to retire here—" She hesitated, and for a moment he thought he detected some tension in her face. "Well, it worked out that it was a good time for me to change jobs, so I looked for something here."

Another measure of how close her family had been. As much as Gerry had loved him, he didn't think the consideration of being close to him had entered into Gerry's decision about where he went to college.

Well, he wouldn't have expected it. Or wanted it, for that matter. Gerry had his chance at playing on a national championship basketball team. Naturally that was all he'd thought of.

Except that Gerry hadn't had that chance. It had been gone in a moment of bad judgment—a moment Mason could have prevented.

A wave of panic went through him. He'd spent most

of his adult life evading being responsible for anyone else's happiness. Now he had the sole responsibility for a child's future. How on earth was he going to handle that?

Alexis turned on her side and pulled the yellow and blue quilt up over her shoulder. Her father had opened the door a few minutes ago to check on her. She'd pretended she was asleep.

He seemed nice. But it was hard to find something to say to him. He looked at her as if he was afraid she'd break.

She closed her eyes. Maybe when she opened them again she'd be back in her bed at school, and none of this would have happened.

She didn't think so, though.

Nice that Jennifer had come over. She was the one who'd suggested reading a chapter of the new book Aunt Shelley had bought for her. They'd sat on the bed together with the book.

And after her bath, Jennifer had known how to spray her hair to get the tangles out. She didn't suppose her father would know that.

Her eyes popped open. She looked at the door. If he'd left it open a little, then she could hear their voices downstairs. That would make her feel better. Safer.

She could get out of bed, tiptoe to the door, open it a crack. But she'd have to get out of bed first.

She'd have to put her feet on the floor. Not that she thought there was anything under the bed, but still—

She could reach out and turn on the lamp. But her arms didn't want to get out from under the quilt.

She shifted, so that she could see the closet door. It was open just a little. She always closed the closet door before she went to bed, but in this strange place, she'd forgotten.

She held her breath, listening for the sounds. She'd slept in lots of different places, and they all had their own sounds. Like Grammie and Grandpa's house in Charleston—cars made bumping sounds when they went over the cobblestones.

This room had a window that looked onto a porch. She'd heard an owl hoot a while ago. Now there was a different sound—a kind of scratching.

She pulled the quilt tighter. Maybe it was a branch. There was a big live oak near the porch. Or a squirrel. Maybe a bird. She didn't need to look.

The scratching came again. Her stomach turned and twisted, as if she was going to be sick. It was nothing. It was nothing.

It wasn't someone's fingers scraping on the glass. It couldn't be.

Grammie always said to pray when you were scared. She tried to think of a prayer. *Now I lay me down to sleep—*

She couldn't go to sleep. She couldn't close her eyes. She had to look.

She'd turn over, very slowly, hiding under the quilt. She'd peek out. She'd see a branch, rubbing against the window. Then she could go to sleep.

Slowly, moving an inch at a time, she rolled over. Holding the quilt over her face, she peeped around it.

The window. A shadow on the glass. Something

reaching out, like an arm trying to reach for her. Trying to get her.

She jumped out of bed and ran, yelling as loud as she could, to the door.

TEN

Mason was sitting, relaxed, in the chair across from Jennifer, finishing their coffee before Jennifer headed home. He was thinking how comfortable this was, when a scream ripped through the house. He was on his feet without knowing how he got there, rushing to the stairs, up them, heart pounding, unable to breathe, hearing Jennifer's footfalls behind him, Alexis—

Alexis flew down the hallway and flung herself into his arms, clutching him with fierce strength, clamping her arms around his neck. Her little body shook with fear, and the shrill cries she uttered seemed to cut right to his heart.

"Alexis, what is it?" His voice was frantic—he ought to calm down, but he couldn't. He had to find out what was wrong. The feel of her in his arms… It was the first time he actually touched her. His heart felt as if it might burst.

He tried to disentangle her arms so he could see her face. "Tell me what happened. Are you hurt?"

No answer, just renewed sobs.

Jennifer knelt next to him. She put her hand on Alexis's back and began stroking it in long, slow movements.

"It's all right, sugar." Her voice was slow, steady, matching the movement of her hand. "It's all right. You're safe now. No one's going to hurt you. We won't let them. You're all right."

Slowly, almost imperceptibly, Alexis began to relax. Jennifer was right, of course, but for an instant he resented the fact that she knew what to do for his child and he didn't.

"It's okay now." He added his reassurances to hers, beating down the need to know what had frightened the child. "No one's going to hurt you. I'm here."

His gaze met Jennifer's, and she gave an approving nod. She went on talking, her voice a calming murmur, until finally Alexis pushed herself back a little, loosening her stranglehold.

"Can you tell us what scared you?" Jennifer stroked the flyaway brown hair.

Alexis swallowed, the muscles of her thin neck working. "Somebody—somebody was on the porch. Trying to get in."

Probably ninety-nine times out of a hundred a parent wouldn't take that seriously. But theirs was no ordinary situation.

He unpeeled Alexis gently, passing her to Jennifer. "Okay, sweetheart. I'm going to go and see. You stay here with Jennifer, all right? You'll be safe with her, I promise."

"We'll be fine." Jennifer wrapped her arms around his daughter. Be careful, the look in her eyes said.

He strode quickly to the room, hands knotting into fists. No one would be there, of course, but he almost hoped there was. He'd like to connect with someone instead of feeling as if he was battling shadows.

In the doorway he felt for the wall switch and flipped it. The bedside lamps came on, bathing the room in a warm yellow glow. The patchwork quilt Jennifer had bought spilled half off the bed in a splash of color, and the book they'd been reading lay facedown on the floor. No indication that this was anything but a child's nightmare, but he couldn't take anything for granted.

He crossed quickly to the porch door, bending over to check the handle. It was still locked, but that flimsy lock wouldn't be difficult to force. He should have thought of that. He switched on the porch light, opened the door and went out.

The spring night air was still cool, but with a hint of the sultriness that would come soon enough. A slight breeze rustled the trees, sending the drapes of Spanish moss dancing.

One of the gnarled branches of the live oak nearest the house crooked toward the window. That must be what Alexis had seen. He couldn't find any indication that anyone had been here.

Still, it was important that Alexis *feel* safe, as well as be safe. He went back into the room to find Jennifer and Alexis watching him from the doorway. Alexis clung to Jennifer's arm, and the sight did something funny to his heart.

"There isn't anyone here, baby girl." The Southern endearment came to his tongue without thought. "But I think maybe you and I should put a heavier bolt on that door. What do you think?"

Alexis's eyes grew wide in her solemn face. Then she nodded.

"Okay." He'd said the right thing, for once. "You girls wait here, and I'll go get my tools."

It was the work of a few minutes to get what he needed from his well-stocked workbench. When he got back to the room, Jennifer and Alexis were both curled up against the headboard of the bed, talking softly.

"Here we go." He knelt at the base of the door, wanting to put the bolt where Alexis could reach it but where, even if someone smashed one of the small panes of glass, he or she wouldn't be able to.

It didn't take long to drill the holes, and by the time he'd finished, Alexis was kneeling beside him. Funny, how good it felt to ask her for a tool, to guide her small hand in fitting the screws into place. In a matter of minutes the new bolt was installed, and he watched as Alexis fastened it, a hint of a smile on her face.

"Good work, you two." Jennifer still sat on the bed. "You know, I think maybe that tree branch—"

"I already saw it," he said. "In the morning, I'll cut it off."

"Good." She smiled at Alexis. "You know, when I was about your age, I didn't like going to sleep in the dark. My dad helped me set up a routine, so I'd know I was all right. First we'd check the closet."

She rose as she spoke, going to look in the closet. To his surprise, Alexis scrambled to her feet and joined her, looking inside solemnly before closing the door.

"What else did you and your daddy do?" Alexis prompted.

"Well, we checked under the bed. Maybe your daddy could do that."

Your daddy. His heart twisted again. "Sure thing," he said cheerfully. He bent and looked under the bed. "All clear."

"And then what?" Alexis didn't seem satisfied yet, but then, she had more to fear than Jennifer would have.

"Well, then we sat on the bed together and said prayers. And then Daddy kissed me, and turned on the porch light so I could see if I needed to. And when he went out, he left the door open a little so I could hear him and my mommy talking downstairs while I was going to sleep."

Alexis looked at him. The ball was in his court. He sat on the edge of the bed and patted a spot next to him. He was almost surprised when she scurried across the room and climbed up beside him.

He cleared his throat. "Is there a special prayer you like to say?"

She nodded. "Grammie taught me now I lay me and God bless." She patted the spot next to her, mimicking what he had done. "Do you want to sit here?"

Jennifer nodded. "I sure do." She sat down on the other side of his child, and unselfconsciously took Alexis's hand.

Seeming to take that as a hint, Alexis slipped her small hand into Mason's and bowed her head.

"Now I lay me down to sleep…" The words to the prayer he'd said as a child came back to him, and he joined in saying them.

"Amen. God bless Grammie and Grandpop, and—"

Alexis stopped. She glanced toward Jennifer. "I don't know what else to say." There was a lost sound in her voice that cut him like a knife.

"How about, 'God bless all the people I love and all the people who love me'?"

Alexis nodded, seeming satisfied, and repeated the words. Then she slid under the covers and snuggled under the quilt.

He followed Jennifer to the door and turned off the bedside lamps. The porch light cast a pattern on the rug. "Is that all right?"

She nodded. "Don't forget to leave the door open a little bit so I can hear you."

"I won't." He stepped into the hall, leaving the door a good foot open. "Good night, sugar."

"Good night."

How long would it be until Alexis called him Daddy? Even a few days ago he wouldn't have thought it possible. Now he wanted to hear that more than anything.

Jennifer wasn't quite sure how she'd ended up going along on the trip to Charleston to see Alexis's grandparents on Sunday. Not that they were really her grandparents, but it was simpler, and probably more reassuring to Alexis, to continue to refer to them that way.

And speaking of grandparents, it was odd that Mason hadn't mentioned his mother in relation to Alexis. Had he told her yet? He certainly should have.

She glanced at his face, intent as he negotiated Sunday traffic in the popular tourist destination. She couldn't ask him with Alexis in the car, but she should bring it up.

He might say it was none of her business, which it wasn't, strictly speaking. But he had dragged her into helping him with his daughter, so he could hardly object if she had questions.

This trip was a good case in point. She hadn't intended to come, but when Alexis simply assumed she would, and when Mason gave her that pleading smile, she couldn't say no.

That was a sobering thought. She'd best find a way to say no to Mason, before she was in so deep that heartbreak was inevitable.

Saying no might have to wait awhile, though. Alexis obviously still welcomed her presence as a buffer to being alone with her father. She could hardly blame the child. She and Mason seemed more comfortable together after the alarms of Friday night, when he'd stepped up so well to his responsibilities, but it had to be awkward still. Alexis had never known a father, even a false one, so she must still be feeling her way.

Jennifer glanced in the rearview mirror to see Alexis in the backseat, looking out at the familiar surroundings. Penny's parents lived, not in Charleston proper, but in the Old Towne section of Mount Pleasant, across the Cooper River from historic Charleston.

Alexis had been exuberant at first, proudly directing them to a restaurant on Shem Creek where they could have lunch. Watching the boats going in and out had provided plenty of distraction during lunch, but when they left the restaurant, Alexis had grown silent.

"Alexis?" Jennifer turned to look at her. "Is everything okay?"

Alexis shrugged, not meeting her gaze. Then... "They're not really my grandparents, are they?"

It was an expression of her fear that they wouldn't love her anymore, and it wrung Jennifer's heart. "You know, I think being grandparents is more about how people feel about each other than whether they're blood kin. Your grandparents love you. That's not going to change."

Mason cleared his throat. "They were so excited when I told them we were coming today. They can't wait to see you."

Alexis seemed to weigh that for a moment, and then the troubled look slipped from her face. "Okay," she said. She leaned forward and pointed. "Their house is one more block. On that side."

Jennifer tried to swallow the lump in her throat. How much harm Penny had done with her deceptions. People had been hurt and would continue to be hurt because of her. Even if she never turned up again...

Was that a reasonable expectation? Penny's parents might have some insight into her probable actions. From what Shelley had said, the police hadn't questioned them much at all, because they'd been so emotionally distraught. Maybe today...

The idea grew. Penny's father was in the early stages of Alzheimer's disease, so it was unlikely he'd be of much help, but maybe her mother would be willing to talk. If only she could learn something, anything, to ease this tension, that would help.

"There's the house." Alexis bounced on the backseat. "Look— That's my grammie looking out the window!"

* * *

Once they were inside the graceful antebellum house and introductions had been made, Jennifer realized that Mrs. Brighton was as much a period piece as her home. Small, as delicate as a piece of fine china, she had to be a good twenty years older than Jennifer's parents.

Penny must have come along late in her parents' marriage, perhaps the child they'd longed for but never though they'd have. Did that help any in understanding why Penny had turned out the way she had?

"Goodness, what am I doing keeping you standing here?" Mrs. Brighton turned from hugging Alexis, cheeks pink with pleasure. "Please, come out in the garden." She stroked Alexis's hair, her hand trembling a little. "Run on out, dear. Your granddad is waiting for you."

Alexis ran through the archway on their right, through a formal living room and out a pair of French doors to the garden that was visible beyond. Characteristic of many Charleston houses, this one sat with its end to the street, its front actually at the side, facing onto an enclosed garden.

"You have a beautiful home," Jennifer said, looking at the fine woodwork of the graceful fireplace.

"Thank you, dear. Too much for the two of us, I'm afraid, but I don't want to uproot my husband at this stage." Worry creased her brow. "He loves it here so. We're fortunate to have such good help. Our dear Lydia always takes Sunday off, but she's left all of Alexis's favorite cookies to have with our tea later."

Jennifer tried to picture Penny in this setting and failed completely. Penny, with her reckless zest for excitement, must have felt stifled in this careful recreation of life as it had once been lived in the south. Had that led her to the wild behavior that had her kicked out of one school after another?

"It's good of you to have us." Mason seemed to be struggling with how to deal with what was admittedly an awkward situation.

"Oh, please." Mrs. Brighton put her hand on his arm, her faded blue eyes filling with tears. "It's you who are good. When we heard the news, we were afraid we'd never seen that dear child again. It would have killed my husband, I know it."

"Don't think that." Mason covered her hand with his, his voice warming. "You're an important part of Alexis's life. I don't want to take anything from her."

Jennifer's throat clogged with tears she was determined not to shed. Here, at least, were people who wanted to do right by Alexis, and who would put her needs first, unlike Penny.

Fury swept through her unexpectedly. Why had Penny taken the child, only to ignore her? It made no sense that a reasonable person could understand.

Jennifer followed Mason and their hostess through the French door, onto a narrow covered veranda and to where Alexis's grandfather sat in a comfortable rocker, Alexis beside him. It was sweet to see them together, Jennifer soon realized. Mr. Brighton sometimes lost the thread of his thought, or stumbled for a word, but Alexis was quick to fill in for him.

Apparently the two of them had a project going with some bird feeders, and Alexis ran back and forth, filling the feeders under his direction, eventually enlisting Mason to help her with some of the higher ones.

Mrs. Brighton rose, smiling at their happy preoccupation. "I'll just bring out the sweet tea and cookies."

This was probably the only chance she'd have to talk with the woman alone. Jennifer got up quickly. "Let me help, please."

Not heeding their hostess's faint protests, she followed her into the house and back to the kitchen.

"Well, dear, maybe you could just arrange those cookies on that glass plate." Penny's mother started setting out glasses on a tray. Frowning a little, she glanced at Jennifer and away again. "If you wouldn't mind… If I could ask you…"

Jennifer turned from washing her hands at the sink. Apparently Mrs. Brighton had been waiting to get her alone, too.

"Please, ask me anything you like."

Emboldened, she nodded. "I wouldn't pry if it weren't for Alexis. It's just that she seems so fond of you already, and I wondered about you and Mason. I mean…" She let that trail off.

Jennifer felt sure that her cheeks had grown pink, but she owed the woman an honest answer. "Mason and I were good friends in college, but then we didn't see each other for ten years. Now— Well, I think we're friends again. It's difficult, in a way, when you knew someone in college." She wanted to get the conversation onto Penny without being too obvious. "I do care about him and Alexis, and if I can help them build a bond together, that will be enough."

Would it? In a moment of clarity, she saw that it wouldn't. She wanted more, but it didn't seem very likely she'd get it.

"You obviously mean a lot to both of them." She smiled gently. "Perhaps…."

"Perhaps," Jennifer agreed. She arranged a row of cookies. "It seems so strange, getting together with the people I was so close to in college. In a way, the years seem to drop away, and yet we've all changed so much. As for Josie—" She paused.

"Alexis's mother." Mrs. Brighton was obviously not one to balk at facts, despite her air of fragility. "Did you know her well?"

"I thought I did. But now I know that she'd kept her pregnancy secret all that time, and it changes how I look on that."

Mrs. Brighton sighed. "Poor girl." She sounded sorrowing, but Jennifer wondered if she'd really accepted the possibility that Penny had killed her friend.

The elderly woman looked at her, almost as if she guessed what Jennifer was thinking. "Did you know our Penny?"

"Not as well," she admitted. "Most of my friends were the kids in Campus Christian Fellowship. Penny wasn't involved with that, but we did live in the same dorm." She took a breath. "I've begun to wish I had known her better. Maybe, if I had, I'd have some idea of what she's going to do now."

Mrs. Brighton nodded, standing as tall as her almost five feet would allow. "I know what you're asking, dear.

Believe me, I have no illusions left about Penny after all these years. You don't have to be afraid to speak."

Her steel backbone was evident beneath her genteel exterior.

"Thank you. I just hoped you might have some insight. She'd expected to get money from Mason to keep silent about Alexis, and when that fell through—" She shrugged, not ready to advertise her part in that. "The police seem to think she'd run away. I'm not so sure."

Penny's mother shook her head slowly, and the desolation in her eyes struck Jennifer to the heart. "If I knew anything that would help to find her, I'd speak, no matter what the results. But I don't."

That seemed to be it, then. "Well, thank you for telling me." She moved quickly to pick up the heavy tray with the frosty pitcher of sweet tea and the glasses before the elderly woman could attempt to carry it.

"One thing." The woman's voice stopped her before she reached the door.

Jennifer looked back. Penny's mother stood at the counter, staring down at the plate of cookies. Then she looked up at Jennifer.

"If Penny thinks she has been wronged, she'll go to any extremes to get even. Any extremes." A shudder went through her. "Be careful, my dear. Please be careful."

ELEVEN

The phone in Jennifer's office rang shortly after the last of the preschool children left on Tuesday. Her breath hitched, as it always seemed to do lately when the phone rang. She stood for a moment with her hand on the receiver and then picked it up.

"Hello?"

As soon as the woman began to speak, she knew it wasn't Penny, and her pulse steadied.

"Miss Pappas, this is Genevieve Rogers, principal at Pine Street Elementary. Mr. Grant left your number as a backup person to call if we couldn't reach him in an emergency."

Her heart jolted painfully. "Alexis— What's wrong? Is she hurt?" *Please, God, please.*

"No, no, she's not injured, but something has upset her." The woman sounded frustrated. "Unfortunately she won't tell us what it is. Since we can't reach her father, if you could come over…"

"Of course. I'm only a few blocks away. I'll be right there." She hung up the phone on the woman's goodbyes and dashed for the stairs.

It wasn't until she was halfway to the school that it occurred to her how odd it was that the principal hadn't been able to reach Mason. In the middle of a workday, surely he was at the office.

Well, she had his cell number. Quickly she pulled out her phone and pressed in the number. Given what the principal had said, she half-expected to reach his voice mail, but he answered almost immediately.

"Mason." Her relief must show in her voice. "The school called me, and—"

"Alexis!" He sounded as if he wanted to jump through the phone. "Is she all right?"

"She's safe, really. But she's very upset and won't tell them why. I'm just pulling into the parking lot now. Where are you?"

"Halfway to Somerville." She thought she heard the shriek of tires. "I'll be there as soon as possible. Jennifer—" His voice choked. "Take care of her, will you? Tell her I'm on my way."

"I will." Her voice choked, too. "Don't worry." She pulled into the visitor's slot. "I'm here now. I'll call you back as soon as I know anything."

She slid out of the car and hurried toward the door. The school office was on the right when she entered the hallway, and she could see Alexis through the plate-glass window. She was huddled in a chair, her face hidden, seeming to ignore the woman who sat next to her.

Jennifer yanked the door open. Alexis looked up at the sound and fairly catapulted herself off the chair and into her arms. Jennifer hugged her, realizing she hadn't been totally convinced she was safe until this moment.

"Sweetheart, it's all right. I'm here now, and Daddy's on his way." She stroked the soft, flyaway hair. "You're going to be fine. I won't leave you."

She sat down, Alexis on her lap, holding her close. Above the child's head, she met the gaze of the other woman. "Miss Rogers?"

"Yes. You're Miss Pappas, I take it." She smiled, but worry still darkened her expression. "I'm glad you're here."

"I was able to reach Alexis's father. He's on his way." She dropped a kiss on Alexis's head. "You hear, sugar? He was on his way to Somerville, but he turned around and he's coming."

Alexis nodded, her sobs seeming to lessen.

"Something apparently happened while the children were outside for lunch recess." Miss Rogers smoothed a strand of dark blond hair behind her ear. She was in her early forties, at a guess, so she had some experience, but she still looked a bit shaken. "We don't know what. The teacher on duty found her huddled against the door, crying hysterically, but she can't or won't tell us what frightened her."

Jennifer stroked Alexis's back, relieved that her sobs had diminished. "Can you tell me about it, sugar? What happened?"

For a moment she thought Alexis wouldn't answer. Then she drew back a little, so that Jennifer could see her tear-drenched eyes.

"She was there. Watching me."

Jennifer's stomach lurched. "Who, Alexis? Who was watching you?"

"Her." The child's mouth twisted. "My…" She stopped, shook her head. "Penny. Penny was standing by the fence, watching me." Her voice trembled on the words, her eyes filling with tears again.

"Honey, are you sure?" Surely even Penny wouldn't be brazen enough to be out there in broad daylight with the police looking for her.

"It was!" Alexis flared up, then flung herself against Jennifer. "Don't let her take me away."

Jennifer wrapped her arms around her, holding her fiercely. "It's all right. No one's going to take you away. But, honey—"

"I know it was." Her voice was muffled against Jennifer's shoulder. "She had on different clothes. Jeans and an old shirt. And her hair was different. But it was her."

"We'll keep you safe, darling. Don't worry." She rested her chin on the top of Alexis's head and looked at the principal.

The woman's eyebrows lifted. "That's the child's mother?"

Somehow she hated having the term applied to Penny. "Foster mother," she said, figuring that was close enough. Undoubtedly Miss Rogers had heard some garbled version of the story by now. "Alexis must be kept away from her at all costs."

Miss Rogers nodded. "Mr. Grant made that clear, and we do have policies in place for this sort of situation. Custody disputes, and that sort of thing."

She knew, only too well. They'd had policies in place at the day-care center in New York, too, and they'd still come close to losing a child, thanks to her stupidity.

Why was Alexis out for recess without someone keeping a close eye on her? That was what she wanted to say, but she didn't have the right. Mason did, though, and he undoubtedly would.

She shifted Alexis's weight so she could reach her bag. "Let me call your daddy, okay? We'll find out how close he is."

Alexis sat up, nodding, and wiped her eyes. The mere mention of her father seemed to give her assurance, and that said good things about their fledgling relationship.

Mason answered so quickly that he must have been driving with his hand on the cell phone. "Is she all right?"

"Alexis is fine," she said carefully, not wanting to start any tears flowing again. "She's sitting right here with me."

"And you have to be careful of what you say." Mason caught on quickly. "It'll probably take me another fifteen or twenty minutes."

"I'll stay right with her. Just check in the office when you get here."

"Right." He clicked off.

"Will he be here soon?" Alexis seemed herself again at the prospect.

"In about twenty minutes." She glanced at Miss Rogers. "Do you think it would be better if Alexis went back to her class and I stayed with her?"

The woman nodded. "An excellent idea. I'm sure Alexis would like to help her class with their science project, and her teacher would be happy to have you there. I'll send her father along to the classroom as soon as he arrives."

Jennifer nodded, satisfied. That would give Miss

Rogers a chance to talk with Mason privately, and being kept busy with her classmates was probably the best thing to distract Alexis right now.

She stood up, taking Alexis's hand. "How about showing me where your classroom is, okay?"

Alexis nodded. "Okay." She looked up at the principal. "Thank you, Miss Rogers."

The principal's face softened in a smile. "You're welcome, Alexis. I'll see you later."

At first when they entered the classroom, Alexis seemed determined to stay by Jennifer's side. But once they'd started working on the science project, Alexis became engrossed in painting the rings for the model of Saturn, and Jennifer was able to move off to a chair near the door.

She watched from there, making a mental note that Alexis was into crafts. Every little bit of information she could gain about the child might help with her adjustment.

She studied that intent little face. Alexis had been terrified at the idea that Penny was watching her. A chill shivered down her spine. Why was Alexis afraid of the woman she'd thought was her mother? Was the fear based on the idea of having Penny back in her life? Or was it based on what Penny might do?

She really needed to talk this through with Mason. She couldn't help him with Alexis when she was working blind. She didn't even know if he'd tried to discuss Penny with Alexis.

Not for the first time, she wondered if Alexis should be seeing a therapist. The disruptions in her young life would be enough to shake someone much older. Should she suggest that to Mason? And if she did, would he withdraw behind that mask of his and think that it wasn't her business?

Someone tapped on the window of the door. She turned. Mason stood there, gesturing to her to come out into the hallway.

With a glance at Alexis, she opened the door. "You'd better come in. I told Alexis I wouldn't leave."

He nodded and slipped inside, his gaze going quickly to his daughter. "She looks okay," he murmured.

"She was pretty shaken when I got here. Did Miss Rogers tell you what she said?" The children were chattering so exuberantly as they worked that she wasn't afraid of being overheard. It was a cheerful, noisy, happy classroom, just the kind she felt most at home in.

Vertical lines formed between Mason's eyebrows. "Alexis thought she saw Penny watching her." He glanced at her, the look questioning. "Surely Penny wouldn't take a risk like that, would she?"

"She's taken plenty of others." Jennifer shivered at the memory of finding Penny in her kitchen. She'd thought her house was safe. It hadn't been.

"Even so—" Mason shook his head as if he were trying to clear it, rather than as if he were saying no. "Alexis is obviously upset at the idea of Penny finding her. Maybe she saw a woman who resembled her and her imagination did the rest."

"She did say—" She stopped, remembering exactly what Alexis had said. "She told me that the clothes were different. And then she said that the hair was different, too. Which it is. You remember, I told the police that Penny had dyed it red. But Alexis couldn't know that."

He seemed to weigh that. "That's true, but did she say the woman had red hair, or just that it looked different?"

"That it looked different." She looked at the child, relieved that Alexis seemed to have shaken off her fears. "I suppose you should talk to her about it at some point, but I think I'd leave it alone for a while."

He looked harassed. "I can't leave it too long. I'll have to tell the police what happened. And whether it was Penny or not, I don't want Alexis left alone for a single minute until she's caught."

"She wouldn't do anything to the child—" Fear clutched her.

Mason's expression was grim. "I still think it's doubtful that she was actually here. But she's not going to have a chance to get anywhere near my daughter." He shook his head. "Although how I'm going to run a business and stay with Alexis all the time when she's not in school, I don't know."

She hesitated only a moment. "Would you consider putting her in the after-school program at church? I think she'd have a good time there, and I can promise you that she'd be well supervised."

"Are you sure?" He looked at her intently. "It seems to me I've already dragged you into my problems enough. I certainly didn't think the school would have to call you when I gave them your number."

"That's what the after-school program is for. We'll be delighted to have Alexis. She can start today if you want. You can drop her off after school and fill out the paperwork then."

"Maybe I should wait until tomorrow. After today's upset—"

"I understand. Whenever you want. And she doesn't have to come every day, you know. Our van will pick her up here after school, and the teachers supervise the children until they're in the van and on their way."

"Sounds good."

And he sounded relieved. Poor Mason—he'd really been pitched into being a single parent, and he had to learn all the things most parents had figured out by this time.

"As for the school calling me—" She shrugged. "I'm just glad I was there. Apparently they tried your home number and your office, but your secretary said you were out of reach."

It occurred to her again how odd that was. She'd been able to reach him quite easily on the cell phone.

"Eva told them she couldn't reach me." Mason said the words slowly, as if seeing how they sounded.

"That's what Miss Rogers said."

His face tightened. "You know, I think I will bring Alexis over after school today. I find I'm going to have to go back to the office."

Apparently Mason found that as odd as she had. "There must be some explanation." Eva hadn't impressed her very favorably on their only meeting, but surely the woman wouldn't deliberately lie when it came to a child's welfare.

"For Eva's sake, I hope so."

Mason's mouth set in a grim line, and all she could think was that she was glad that expression wasn't directed toward her.

Mason glanced at his watch as he drove toward the office. Enrolling Alexis in the after-school program hadn't taken as long as he'd feared it might, and he had plenty of time for what he had to do.

Getting Alexis settled after her earlier fright might have been difficult, but Jennifer had smoothed the way, as she'd been doing ever since he'd told her that Josie's child might be his.

It wasn't fair to her, involving her so deeply in his troubles. There couldn't be a future for them, no matter what he might feel for her.

He'd messed up enough lives already. He wouldn't add Jennifer to the count.

He could, however, deal with Eva. He found his jaw clenching as he pulled into his parking space behind the building. It was long past time for a confrontation between them. He'd put up with her lack of respect out of old habit, but Alexis was different. Eva couldn't be allowed to play games with his daughter's safety.

He unlocked the back door and hurried up the stairs that led to his office. In moments he was storming into the outer office.

Eva looked up from her desk, eyes wide. "Mason. I didn't know you were here."

"Did you know where I was?" He rapped out the question.

She blinked several times. "You went to Somerville this afternoon, didn't you?"

He leaned on her desk, planting his hands on its edge. "Why did you tell my daughter's school that you couldn't reach me?"

Again she blinked, slowly this time, looking for all the world like an aged turtle. "I don't know what you mean."

"My daughter's school called this afternoon, trying to reach me. You told them I was out of touch. Why? It was important."

She drew back a little from the anger in his voice. "Important? The business your father started is important. You were supposed to be in Somerville this afternoon. Didn't you go?"

The woman was impossible. "Did you hear me? This was an emergency involving my daughter. If Jennifer Pappas hadn't thought to call my cell phone, I still wouldn't have known about it."

"Jennifer Pappas." She said the name as if it tasted sour. "What business is it of hers?"

"It was your business, Eva. You are my secretary. I left this number with the school because you always know where I am. And when my daughter was in trouble—"

"Stop calling her that!" She shot to her feet suddenly, sending the chair rolling toward the wall behind her. "How could you? How could you bring that child here, dishonoring your family name?"

He felt the blood drain from his face. "Alexis is my daughter."

"Your illegitimate child. What would your father say

if he knew she was living in your house, probably taking your name—"

"You're fired." He dropped the words in quietly. He didn't raise his voice. He didn't need to.

She gaped at him for a long moment. "You—you can't fire me. Your father promised me this job was mine—"

"My father has been dead for over ten years. Grant's Sporting Goods is my company, something you've never seemed to understand. Well, understand this. Your position is terminated as of right now. Pack your personal things and get out."

"I— You can't. I won't go—"

He reached across her desk, picked up the telephone, and punched in the number for security. "Joe? Come up to my office now. I need you to escort an employee from the premises."

"Yes, sir."

He hung up. Looked at her.

Her mouth worked as if she'd give anything to speak, but she didn't. She dragged a stationery box from the closet and began to throw things in it.

He watched her impassively, not letting himself give in to the urge to look at the portrait of his father over her desk. He ought to give it to her, but he could imagine how quickly that news would get around town.

By the time the security guard arrived, Eva was ready. She stalked toward the door, carrying the box. Joe made an effort to take it for her, but she jerked away from him.

Something twisted inside him. She had to go, but he hadn't needed to call security. He should—

She turned at the door, her expression venomous.

"Your father was right about you. You never amounted to anything, and you never will."

The door closed behind her. He took a breath, not sure how long it had been since he breathed. Then he walked to the wall, lifted the portrait down and shoved it into the closet.

TWELVE

Jennifer was smiling as she turned from the gym door and headed back toward her office. She'd have something good to report to Mason when he came to pick up his daughter. After several days of the after-school program, Alexis seemed to be settling in very nicely.

She'd been Jennifer's little shadow at first, tagging along at her heels and ignoring every effort to interest her in an activity. But eventually the shadow of fear left her eyes.

Brandon had been a big help. Even though Kate's son was a year younger than Alexis, the two had formed a surprising bond. Brandon liked showing her the ropes at the program, and Alexis seemed to enjoy playing the big sister. Maybe it was partly because they were both only children. Whatever the reason, Jennifer was pleased.

She pushed open her office door and headed for the desk. She'd been paying so much extra attention to Alexis that she'd let her daily reports slide. Maybe now she could start getting back to normal.

Normal—wouldn't that be nice? Things had been so quiet that she could almost believe the police were right, and that Penny was far, far away from here by now.

Certainly that would be the sensible course of action for a fugitive. She thought about Mrs. Brighton's words. Penny's mother didn't seem to think Penny was likely to be sensible, but she'd apparently seen little of her in recent years. Maybe…

Running footfalls, and before she could get up the door burst open. Mason charged toward her desk. "Alexis— Where is she? Why isn't she with you?"

His anxiety was almost contagious, even though she knew exactly where Alexis was. "Mason, she's fine. She's playing in the gym. Why are you so upset?"

He didn't answer, just turned and made for the gym. Her concern building, she hurried after him.

She caught up with him by the time he reached the gym door, and she put her hand on his arm. "Take it easy. She's fine, so don't rush in there and scare her."

The tension in him didn't ease, but at least he opened the door and went in quietly. She slipped in behind him, letting the door close.

"You see?" she murmured.

Alexis dribbled down the basketball court with Brandon dancing around her, trying to steal the ball, while several other third and fourth graders made a spirited effort to look like a basketball team.

Jennifer felt Mason's anxiety ebb away at the sight of his daughter. And probably especially when he saw the six-foot-four college boy who was shouting encouragement as he ran alongside the kids.

"She's okay." The words came out on a sigh of relief. "Who is your helper?"

"Seth Martin. He's our intern from the college this semester, and he's really working out well. The kids just love him." She glanced at his face, noting the lines of strain. "He knows about Penny, Mason. Believe me, he won't let any unauthorized person anywhere near Alexis."

"Good." He focused on Brandon. "That little guy looks familiar."

"You remember Brandon, Kate's boy." She smiled. "The two of them have become friends. It's really nice to see."

"Yes." He turned toward her, leaning against the door. "I'm sorry I snapped at you, but there's something I have to show you."

His face tightened on the words, and apprehension snaked down her spine.

"What is it? What's happened?"

"This came in today's mail." He passed her a folded sheet of copy paper.

She opened it, feeling as if something ugly was going to jump out. It did, in a way.

It was typed, obviously on a computer, short and to the point.

You still owe me. Don't think the kid is safe at school, or at that church program, either. There's nowhere I can't get to her. Get the money ready, or I might just have to take her back.

It wasn't signed.

Jennifer fought down the fear. Being afraid wouldn't help. "Have you talked to the police yet?"

"Not yet. All I could think was getting here and seeing that Alexis is all right. I'll give them a call now and—"

"Hey! You're here." Alexis ran toward them. "We don't have to go home yet, do we? Come and play."

Mason's obvious pleasure at Alexis's greeting warred with that foolish reluctance of his to step onto a basketball court.

"Go on," she urged. "Play with your daughter."

Alexis grabbed his arm. "Come on. Please? I want you to play."

He wouldn't be able to resist that, she realized. He might turn her down if she asked him, but he wouldn't want to disappoint Alexis.

Sure enough, his face relaxed in a smile. "All right. Just for a few minutes."

Jennifer folded the paper and slid it into the pocket of her chinos. Mason had to talk to the police about this, of course, but building his relationship with his daughter was even more important.

Fortunately he was dressed casually—khaki pants, a knit polo and running shoes. As soon as he reached the floor, Seth tossed him the ball, and he caught it with an ease that showed he hadn't forgotten.

In a moment the two men and the kids were engrossed in a noisy game. She leaned against the wall, watching, remembering the ten-years-ago Mason, and how she'd gone to every game just for the pleasure of seeing him play.

It was good that he was doing that again. He was loosening up even as she watched, and her heart warmed. He shouldn't give up something he'd loved as much as basketball out of some foolish notion that he'd let his team down.

The fear was still there, underneath, but she could hold it at bay for a moment or two. Seeing Mason and Alexis play together was a glimpse of what life could be like for them one day, when this was all over.

Her heart swelled until she thought it would burst, and then determination hardened inside her. Penny had to be stopped, no matter what it took.

Mason fought to keep a calm facade as Rivers and Paterson pored over the latest message from Penny at the house that evening. They'd already read him a lecture on his failure to bring it directly to them the moment he received it.

He couldn't regret his actions, though. The time he'd spent in the church gym, playing basketball with his daughter, had been golden. Seeing the intent look on her face when she shot the ball, recognizing an innate athletic ability that just might have come from him had moved him more than he could say. They'd actually had fun together, and Alexis had looked freer than he'd ever seen her.

He couldn't ignore the pure pleasure he'd found at playing again, either. He'd gotten quickly into a rhythm with Seth, the college kid, and found he was wondering why he'd stayed away so long from a sport he'd once loved. Seen in the context of his whole life, one missed shot didn't loom as large as it once had.

Nikki Rivers looked up from the sheet of paper they'd spread on the coffee table in his living room.

"Your daughter—is she here, Mr. Grant? Be better, I think, if she didn't overhear this conversation."

"She won't. She's up in her room, showing Miss Pappas her new computer. Jennifer will keep her occupied until we're finished."

The woman nodded, but there seemed to be a slight reservation in her eyes.

Was she wondering about his relationship with Jennifer? Well, the truth was that he wondered, too.

He'd talked her into joining them for a pizza after work, and then into coming to the house to keep an eye on Alexis while he consulted the police.

Not that he'd had to do too much convincing. Jennifer wouldn't turn him down, not where his daughter's safety or happiness was concerned.

He knew he was taking advantage of her, but what else could he do? She was the only other person Alexis trusted in her new life. Or he trusted, for that matter.

Oh, he could have turned to Kate, he supposed, or one of the others from the old gang, but it wouldn't have been the same. And maybe it was best if he not look too closely at why that was.

"Well?" He was growing impatient at their lengthy scrutiny of the letter. It didn't seem that complicated to him. "What do you think?"

"We'll want to let our experts have a look," Paterson said. "Still, a computer printout doesn't tell us much. The envelope is postmarked locally, but that doesn't mean she's still in town."

"If she was the one who wrote it," Rivers added.

Mason stared at her. "Not Penny? Of course it had to

be Penny? Who else would do this? Or know enough to do it?" His jaw clenched. "She has to be watching us. She even knew that I'd put Alexis in the after-school program."

"Certainly Penny Brighton seems the most likely person, but we have to cover all the bases." Paterson's tone was soothing. "Believe me, there are plenty of rumors flying around town about Penny Brighton and about your situation. It's always possible that some nut might try to cash in on it. That sort of thing happens more often than you'd believe."

He'd been managing to ignore the probability that people were talking, but that brought it home to him. He couldn't say he liked it, but it bothered him less than he'd have expected.

"It seems unlikely to me, but I suppose you have to look at everything."

Rivers seemed to be regarding him thoughtfully. "Is there anyone you can think of who might do something like this? Other than Brighton, that is?"

Eva Morrissey popped into his mind. She had what she'd consider good reason to hold a grudge against him, and she'd made her attitude clear. Still, did he really want to set the police on her?

"Well, Mr. Grant?" Rivers was on to his hesitation instantly.

"I found it necessary to fire my secretary recently. I suppose it's possible she might hold a grudge, but I can't believe she'd do something like this."

"Would she have the necessary knowledge?"

"I suppose so." Reluctantly, he gave Eva's name and address, which Paterson jotted down in a notebook.

"You seem to have a lot of confidence in Miss Pappas," Rivers commented.

"Yes. I do." Anger at the insinuation made his voice sharp. "I have every confidence in her."

"I'm not making any accusations." Rivers lifted her eyebrows. "We understand you were friends in college, but you hadn't seen anything of her until the reunion last year."

"She hasn't changed," he said shortly. "Instead of wasting time on my friends, suppose we talk about what you're doing to resolve this."

"I know it must not seem that way to you, but we are working the case hard." Paterson frowned. "Something rather odd has turned up in another case that seems to connect with Miss Brighton. There's a chance we'll get a break in that direction."

"Are you talking about Cornell Rutherford?" Everyone in town had been astonished when the college administrator had been arrested in connection with a point-shaving scheme. Kate seemed to believe he and Penny had some connection, but it seemed like a reach to him.

"We really can't discuss it," Rivers said repressively. "Just be assured we're not idle." She glanced around the room. "As another precaution, have you considered putting an alarm system in?"

"The company's coming tomorrow to do the installation." That was something he probably should have done long ago. "And my daughter will not be left alone for a minute until you catch that woman."

Rivers rose, signaling the end to the conversation, and she and Paterson started moving toward the door.

"We're doing all we can," she said again. "You have to trust us on this, Mr. Grant."

He supposed they were, at least the way they saw it. He just wasn't sure that was going to be enough.

Jennifer watched the expression on Mason's face as he came downstairs from tucking his daughter in bed. There was a softness and openness there that she hadn't seen since their early years in college. Having a daughter was changing Mason in ways he probably didn't recognize and couldn't have imagined a short time ago.

His gaze caught Jennifer's and he gave her a rather guilty smile. "I hope I'm not spoiling her, but she really loves that new computer."

"If you are, it's only natural. Goodness, kids seem born knowing all about computers these days. Did you know her teacher even has a Web page for her class?"

"Times have changed." He came and sat down opposite her. "If it hadn't been for our college class site that you girls started, I wonder whether everything would have come out about Josie and Penny?"

"Probably. Eventually, anyway. Once Josie's body was discovered, the rest was bound to follow. The contacts we made just helped move things along."

She probably should be leaving. Maybe should have left once Mason put Alexis to bed. She'd been hoping he'd want to share what the police said, but apparently not.

"I should go—" She moved as if to rise.

"Not yet." Mason waved her back in her chair. "You deserve to hear what the police had to say, little though it is."

She sank back in the chair. He was going to confide in her. "I suppose the letter doesn't really bring them any closer to finding Penny."

"No. I didn't think it would, but they can't ignore it." He frowned. "They even suggested—"

She lifted her eyebrows when he stopped. "Suggested what?"

"That it might have been written by someone other than Penny, someone who's just trying to cash in on the situation." He rubbed the crease between his brows. "I guess it hadn't occurred to me that my troubles were quite so well known."

"I'm afraid that's inevitable. You're a prominent man in a small town." That reminded her of something she'd wanted to ask him. "About the rumors—is there any chance your mother might hear?"

His face tightened. "If she did, it wouldn't mean anything to her. She has what the doctors call a form of senile dementia. She gets along all right with plenty of everyday tasks, but she's living in the past for the most part."

"You haven't told her about Alexis?" Obviously Mason's relationship with his parents was a lot different than hers, but she'd still think he'd want to tell her.

"No." His face seemed to close. "It's not likely she'd understand me, and if through some chance she did— well, it wouldn't be pleasant."

"I'm sorry. I guess I just can't imagine not having a close relationship with my folks. My dad has stood by me through some rough times."

Now, she thought. Now was the time to tell Mason

about what happened to her in New York. She knew him well enough to know he'd understand.

She looked at him, noting the lines of strain in his face. Her heart clenched. Was she right to unload this on him now?

"There were a couple of other things the police said." He was frowning, and there seemed to be some constraint in his manner. "They hinted at a relationship between Penny and Cornell Rutherford. Seemed to think something might come to light there."

"Rutherford?" She went through what she knew about the scandal involving the man. That sort of thing was hard on a college. "I don't see how they could have been connected, although—"

"Although what?" Mason's face went on alert.

"Well, I don't know how many people knew this, but when we were in school, the girls used to say not to have any private meetings with the man."

"He hit on coeds?"

She shrugged. "Never on me, and I have no idea whether the rumors were true or not. Even if they were, it's a stretch to assume he had anything to do with Penny."

Mason nodded. "I agree. I'm not counting on anything turning up there that will help, but I suppose the police have to turn over every rock."

"I guess." She frowned. "You said there were a couple of things that they brought up."

"I told you they speculated about someone else writing that note. They wanted to know if there was anyone I know who would have the information that was in the note. I had to tell them about Eva."

"I see." He'd never told her exactly what transpired between him and the secretary, but it couldn't have been good. "You couldn't very well keep it a secret. I'd think they'd be discreet about looking into her."

"I hope so." His gaze evaded hers. "Rivers pointed out that some of the people who are my friends now I hadn't seen much in the ten years since graduation."

It took a moment for the truth to dawn. "You mean, me." Pain clutched at her heart. "You can't believe that I—"

"No, of course I don't. I just thought you should know. I don't believe it for an instant."

But there was something—some very faint shadow of doubt—that colored his voice.

She tried to swallow the pain. Odd. Being suspected by the police—she actually knew how that felt. But she didn't suppose she'd be telling Mason about it anytime soon.

She got up. "Well, it's getting late. I'd better be on my way."

He didn't make any effort to dissuade her. He walked with her to the door, but when she started to open it, he put his hand over hers. "Jennifer, wait. I don't want you to think that I don't trust you. Really."

She managed a smile as she looked up at him. "Thank you." He probably believed what he was saying, but she'd seen the shadow of doubt in his face.

He touched her cheek then, his fingers featherlight. "You've been a rock through all of this. I can't thank you enough."

"It's okay." It was hard to speak, the way her heart was thudding. When he touched her, she couldn't think, let alone form a coherent sentence.

But the bottom line was, he did doubt. And if they couldn't trust each other, how could they possibly be more to each other than they already were?

THIRTEEN

Jennifer sat at the kitchen table, nursing a mug of hot chocolate between her hands. It wasn't really hot chocolate weather, but she found it soothing, especially when she had something on her mind.

Mom had always prescribed hot chocolate for a troubled mind. If she were here now, she'd be sitting across from Jennifer, ready to listen.

"What's going on out here?" Dad came in, running a hand over sleep-ruffled, iron-gray hair. "Can't sleep?"

She shook her head. "Just one of those nights. I'm sorry if I woke you."

He crossed to the stove, sniffed the pan of cocoa and poured out a mug for himself. "You didn't, exactly." He came and sat down across from her. "Call it parent's intuition. Your mom's was much more highly developed than mine is, but I'm trying." He patted her hand. "You must be missing your mom."

"I guess I am. You?"

"Only every day." He smiled. "I know I'm not Mom, but I'm here if you want to talk."

"Thanks, Dad." She almost said no, but that wasn't fair to Dad, who was trying to help.

"You're worried about this whole business with Mason Grant and his child, aren't you?"

She nodded. "Mason. Little Alexis. Poor Josie." She shivered. "Penny."

"Hard to believe someone you knew could turn out that way." Dad shook his head. "How is the little girl doing? How anybody could do that to a child—"

"She seemed really withdrawn at first, but she's been coming out a bit. Tonight, when she was showing me how her computer works, she was the most animated I've ever seen her."

"That's a good sign, isn't it? You must be getting through to her."

"I'm not doing much. It's her father who has to reach her."

"You're helping." He patted her hand. "I know you, Jennifer. If anyone can help that child, you can."

She closed her fingers around his strong hand, wondering how often she'd done that over the years. "Thanks for the vote of confidence. It means a lot that you've always had faith in me."

"Well, of course I do. I'm your father."

She thought of Mason's words about his father. "That's not always the case. Mason's father made him think his entire life that he wasn't worth anything compared to his older brother."

"That's a bad thing to do to a child. He didn't do right by either of them in that case."

She hadn't thought of it that way. "I guess so. A lot

of things might have turned out differently if he'd been able to love both his sons."

"It's tough for a man to become a good father if he didn't have a pattern to follow. Mason's lucky he has you to help him."

"I guess." She stared down into the dregs of her hot chocolate. "It's just— I guess I'm afraid that, if I get too close, I'm going to end up getting hurt."

Dad's fingers closed warmly around her hand. "You know, I think I can tell you exactly what your mother would say to that."

She looked at him, startled. "You can?"

He patted her cheek. "Your mother would say exactly what she lived. That it's never a mistake to love, no matter what the risk is."

The soft words seemed to pummel her heart. Dad was right. That was exactly what she would have said.

"Mom was a strong woman." She had to speak around the lump in her throat. "I'm not sure I'm as brave as she was."

Jennifer was still struggling with her feelings as she made her way into the pew beside her father for the Sunday morning worship service. She sank onto the padded seat, her gaze following the arched columns upward to the soaring ceiling.

Guide me, Father. I don't know what to do with these feelings that I have. Getting to know Mason all over again has been so good, and helping him with Alexis is the most satisfying thing I can imagine. But I can't be in love with him, can I?

Her heart seemed to fill with the answer she'd been denying. She was in love with Mason. She loved his daughter. What was she going to do about that?

Nothing. That was the answer. She could do nothing about it. Mason seemed determined not to risk falling in love, and she didn't see that changing.

Help me to accept, Father. Help me be content with whatever I can do for Mason and Alexis, and guide my steps.

She sensed movement beside her and turned to see Mason and Alexis sliding into the pew next to her. Her heart seemed to stop beating for a moment before it returned to normal and she could smile.

"Good morning." She hoped her voice didn't express surprise. This was the first time she'd seen Mason at worship in months.

"Hi." Alexis squeezed past Mason so that she could sit next to Jennifer. "I knew you'd be here."

"I sure am." She touched Alexis lightly on the shoulder. "Alexis, this is my father."

Alexis held out her small hand, to have it engulfed in Dad's large one. "I'm glad to meet you, Mr. Pappas."

Someone—her grandmother, probably—had made sure that no one would ever find fault with her manners.

Dad's smile was as warm as his heart. "I'm very glad to meet you, Alexis. Jennifer talks about you a lot."

Alexis flushed a little, darting a sidelong look at Jennifer.

Dad shook hands with Mason, and she thought she detected a little reservation in his manner. In spite of

Dad's advice about it never being a mistake to love, he obviously didn't want to see her get hurt.

But he'd been right. Getting hurt was the risk you had to take to love. It was too bad that Mason couldn't seem to see that.

Organ music began, and the buzz of people greeting one another subsided to low-voiced conversations and murmured prayers. Mason's gaze caught hers, a little amused. "You're astonished to see me here. Admit it."

"Not astonished." She could feel her cheeks grow warm. "Maybe just a little surprised."

"I'm not such a heathen as all that," he said. He glanced at Alexis, who was engrossed in a rebus on her children's bulletin. "My daughter just naturally assumed we'd be in church this morning. And—" He paused, his expression sobering.

"And what?" Her voice was soft.

"Maybe it's the effect of fatherhood. I guess I'm feeling the need to look for some spiritual help."

She remembered what he'd said to her once, about God not listening when he prayed. Her heart twisted.

"God will give you what you need," she murmured as the organ burst into the prelude. "And I'll be praying, too."

By the time they'd walked over to Fellowship Hall for the coffee hour after the service, Jennifer had convinced herself that she would not betray her feelings for Mason. She had herself under control, and whatever happened, Mason must never know that she longed for anything more than friendship.

If he guessed the truth, it would make the situation incredibly awkward and difficult. How would she be able to help Alexis then?

She accepted coffee and a peanut-butter cookie, glad to see that Mason appeared to be visiting in a very natural manner with the other parishioners. She stepped away from the serving table, and in a moment he'd worked his way through the crowd to her.

"Alexis has linked up with Brandon." He nodded to where the two of them sat on folding chairs, feet swinging and napkins filled with cookies on their laps.

"It's nice to see them together. She acts like a typical big sister with him."

He nodded. "Maybe she's missed having siblings. Among a lot of other things." His mouth tightened.

He was feeling guilty again, obviously, and that saddened her. He couldn't have done anything when he hadn't even known his child existed.

"Plenty of children grow up fine without siblings," she pointed out. "Whatever else went wrong, Alexis had a lot of love from Penny's parents."

"More than she'd have had from mine if the situation had been different."

"You can't change the past. You can only—"

She stopped at a tug on her sleeve.

One of her after-school children stood there. "Miss Jennifer, I have a note for you."

"Thank you, Joseph." She automatically took the folded paper the boy handed her. "From your mother?"

He shook his head, fidgeting a little as if he wanted to dash off to the cookie table. "Just a lady. She asked if I knew you, and I said yes, so she said would I give it to you."

Her nerves tensed, and her gaze met Mason's. He turned to the boy. "Where did you see this lady?"

Joseph gestured vaguely. "Out there. In the hall, when I went to the restroom."

"What did she look like?" Mason was obviously making an effort to keep his voice calm. "Can you tell us?"

But their luck ran out. Joseph shrugged. "Just a lady. Can I go, Miss Jennifer?"

"Yes. Thank you, Joseph."

Mason frowned as the boy scampered away. "If we'd probed a little more, maybe he'd have remembered something."

"He's not a very noticing child." The paper felt as if it were burning her fingers. "It's either from Penny, or it's not." She flipped it open before she could lose her nerve.

A computer-generated letter, like the last one. Probably the police would be able to make nothing out of this, either. The words—

Her breath caught. *You've been after him since college, but you're nothing to him but a convenience, helping with his kid. Get out of my way if you don't want to get hurt.*

Her instinct was to tear it up, hide it, anything but show it to Mason. But it was too late. He'd already taken it from her hand.

It was too late for a lot of things. She'd keep trying to hide her feelings, because that was the only choice she had. But even if Mason said he didn't believe it, Penny's words would make him wonder. And things wouldn't be the same between them.

* * *

Mason jolted wide-awake in the night, heart pounding. For an instant he couldn't think beyond the racing of his heart. Then he knew. Alexis.

He was out of bed in an instant, racing for the door. Something had wakened him. Maybe some sound that he couldn't remember. Alexis…

He charged down the hall. The door to her room stood ajar. He shoved it open and plunged inside. The bed was empty.

Terror. There was no other word for it, and in that instant he knew what she'd come to mean to him.

"Alexis!"

Fear choked his voice.

If Penny had gotten in—but how could she? The alarm system was activated. The porch doors were closed and bolted. Nothing looked out of place in the room.

He'd call the police. But even as he turned toward the door, Alexis appeared, hair tousled from sleep, rubbing her eyes. She stared at him.

Two steps and he was close enough to drop to his knees, grab her and fold her close in his arms. "You're okay. You're here."

She felt stiff against him, and he knew he was overdoing it. But it was going to take a moment for it to sink in. She was safe.

He forced himself to draw back a little. "I'm sorry if I scared you. But I woke up and came to check on you, and you were gone."

"I just went to the bathroom."

He gave a laugh that came out a little shaky. "I know

that now. It just scared me when I saw that you weren't in your bed."

She seemed to consider that, her face solemn. "Would you miss me if I weren't here?"

His heart twisted until he thought it would break. "I would miss you unbearably." He stroked a strand of fine brown hair away from her face. "I didn't know you for most of your life, but you're still my daughter. I love you and I never want to be without you."

What would Jennifer advise in this situation? He was probably putting too much pressure on Alexis.

"I guess you don't love me yet," he said carefully. "But I hope you will sometime."

For a long moment she didn't respond. Then she put her arms around him and hugged him. He hugged her back, very gently, trying not to let tears well in his eyes.

He'd never imagined feeling a love like this. It was so strong it scared him. If he ever let her down, he wouldn't be able to live with himself.

FOURTEEN

"Can I carry something in for you, Jennifer?" Steff Kessler popped her head into the kitchen, when Jennifer was getting coffee and brownies ready to serve. From the living room came the laughter and chatter of the other four women in their little group of college friends.

They'd been getting together at least once a month, sometimes more often, since their class reunion had brought them all back to Magnolia Falls. Tonight was Jennifer's turn to host.

"Thanks, Steff. Do you want to take that tray of brownies? I have a cheese-and-fruit platter ready in the fridge to get out."

"Sounds good." Steff picked up the serving dish. "Usually I can avoid the sweet stuff, but everything that's been happening lately has me so stressed I head straight for the chocolate."

"It's a good thing I had time to make brownies this afternoon, then." At least it had distracted her from the note that had appeared at the coffee hour. She led the way back into the living room, carrying the cheese tray in one hand and the coffeepot in the other. "Chocolate is good for what ails you."

"Only if you're not allergic to it." Lauren Owens spoke in her soft New Orleans drawl.

"So says the nutritionist," Kate said. "I don't care whether it's good for me or not, I want one." She snatched a double-chocolate walnut brownie from the tray before Steff could put it down.

"What ails Steff that she's trying to treat with chocolate?" Cassie Winters pushed a strand of red hair behind her ear as she took a handful of grapes. As a P.E. teacher, Cassie usually managed to eat healthily.

For a moment Jennifer almost envied her. Like Steff, she'd been treating stress with junk food lately.

"You know." Steff sat down, crossing her long legs with the elegant grace she always displayed. "This business about Penny. It's touched all of us, one way or another. Don't tell me the rest of you haven't been losing sleep over it."

Jennifer looked around the circle of faces, realizing that Steff was right. Everyone, it seemed, had gone through trouble this past year, most of it connected in one way or another with the discovery of Josie's body.

Dee Owens, Lauren's sister, nodded. "I try not to let it affect me, but it feels as if this situation has been dragging on forever. I don't understand why the police can't catch up with Penny if she's still in the area. Or is that just a rumor?"

There was no reason to keep back what she knew from her friends, and every reason to be sure they were on their guard. How did she know where Penny might strike next?

"She's still here, I'm afraid. In fact, she was apparently at the church this morning."

That caused the sensation she'd known it would. Kate put down her glass of sweet tea so abruptly that it sloshed onto the coffee table. "Are you sure? How could she be?" She mopped up the spill with her napkin.

"She handed one of the children a note for me." She shivered again at the thought of that woman being so close to one of the children for whom she felt responsible.

"No!" Steff leaned forward. "What was it? Another threat?"

She nodded. "Basically telling me to stay out of her way. Or else."

"The woman has to be crazy," Kate declared.

"She's a murderess." Steff's voice grew dark. "I'm certain she's responsible for my brother's death, even if it can never be proved. He didn't drown by accident that night at the lake."

For a moment there was silence. Everyone remembered that senior picnic, and the tragedy that broke it up. Steff's brother, Adam, dying so soon after his sudden elopement with Penny.

Dee shook her head. "I just don't understand how she could have done all the things we think she did without help."

"Mason says the police think Cornell Rutherford was involved with her in some way." There seemed no reason to keep that from them, either. "He asked if I remembered anything, and all I could tell him was that women students knew to avoid being alone with him."

"Penny didn't." Cassie's words had everyone turning

to look at her. "Well, don't look at me as if I'm spilling a state secret."

"If you knew something about Penny and Rutherford, why didn't you say so before?" Steff's tone was sharp.

Cassie shrugged. "To tell you the truth, I'd forgotten about it. And anyway, I don't really know anything. It's just that, when you mentioned it, a memory popped into my mind."

"What memory?" Steff prompted.

"I happened to be in the corridor where Rutherford's office was one afternoon." She frowned. "It must have been in January or February, because it was after I missed all those classes when I had the flu, and I was trying to get make-up work scheduled. Anyway, I saw that the blind was pulled down on his office door. I started to walk away, when the door opened. Penny came out." She paused. "Sidled out, is more like it. And the expression she wore— Well, it was like the cat that's been in the cream pot."

"Are you sure you're not just imagining things after the fact?" Kate asked.

Cassie shrugged. "I was too busy with my own worries to think about it at the time. But if she was connected with Rutherford, maybe the police will be able to get something out of him."

"Maybe." She should pass this information on, little though she wanted to talk to the police again. "Do you mind if I tell the detectives about this?"

"Of course not." Cassie seemed to shiver. "We've all suffered from this. We all want to see Penny caught. If nothing else, we owe it to Josie."

Heads nodded. Jennifer looked around the circle of

friends, her heart warming. If nothing else good came of all this, she had her friends back again. That was something rare and important.

Alexis bent over the jigsaw puzzle that was spread out on a table in the corner of the crafts room. This was a good thing to do if you wanted to think, 'cause no one would bother you.

Only she guessed she was worrying, not thinking. If she knew what to do—

"Hey, what're you doing?" Brandon popped up at her elbow. He leaned across to fit a piece into the puzzle. "You missed some."

She wanted to tell him to go away. But if he was there, maybe she could stop thinking about the ugly thing that had appeared on her computer.

Brandon elbowed her. "What's wrong?"

"Nothing."

He looked at her for a minute. "You look as if something's wrong."

She scowled. But maybe… "Your mom's going to get married again, right?"

"Yeah. To Parker. He's cool." Brandon tried another piece.

"So, how do you know this Parker guy really likes you? I mean, it's not as if he knew you all your life." It wasn't the same, but it was sort of as if what was happening to her.

Brandon considered a minute, and then he shrugged. "Some of the guys my mom dated pretended they liked me, but I could always tell. Parker—he treats me like a real person. He does things with me, even when Mom's not there. That means he likes me, doesn't it?"

"I guess."

"Another thing." He grinned. "One time I climbed a tree Parker told me not to, and the branch broke, and I fell. He grabbed me so hard I thought he was mad about the branch. But he just hugged me really, really tight. So I knew."

That was like what her father had done when he found her bed empty. So maybe that meant he did love her.

"Yeah, I think you're right." She slid a puzzle piece into place, feeling better.

Brandon shoved a scrap of paper at her. "Here. I wrote down my mom's e-mail. She said it's okay if we e-mail each other."

All of a sudden she had a bad taste in her mouth. "I don't know if I'm going to use the computer very much."

"Why not? I thought you said it was great."

She shrugged. "I dunno."

"But why?" Brandon sounded as if he'd keep bugging her and bugging her if she didn't tell him something.

She glanced around to make sure Miss Molly, the crafts teacher, was at the other side of the room. "You have to promise not to tell."

Brandon's eyes got round. "Tell what?"

"Promise," she whispered.

"Okay, I promise. I won't tell anybody."

There was a lump in her throat. She wanted to tell, but she was afraid to. But Brandon was safe, wasn't he?

"I had an e-mail from her. From Penny."

"The one the police are looking for?"

She nodded. "You know she said she was my mother, but she wasn't."

It made her feel good to say that. She'd always known Penny didn't love her, not like Grammie did, not like her friends' mothers loved them.

"You should tell your dad." Brandon seemed certain.

"I can't." She thought about the things the e-mail had said, and it made her want to shrivel up like a dead bug. "I can't. I mean, it's not like he ever wanted to have a daughter. He never even knew about me."

"So what? He's your dad."

"But if he never wanted me, maybe if I'm too much trouble, he'll send me away." That was what the e-mail said. She didn't want to believe it, but how could she know?

"I still think you should tell him." Brandon sounded determined. "Right away, so he can tell the cops."

"I don't know. Maybe." If only she could be sure. "But you can't tell anybody. Remember. You promised."

Brandon didn't look happy, but he nodded. "I won't tell."

Mason hurried down the stairs to the after-school center on Monday. He was early to pick up Alexis, but that was intentional. He had to talk to Jennifer.

There hadn't been an opportunity the previous day to discuss that note that had been handed to her at the coffee hour. He hadn't missed the embarrassment she'd shown. He had to tell her what the police had said, and he also needed to find some way of easing her feelings about Penny's insinuations.

He rapped lightly on her half-open door and went inside. Jennifer looked up, and he thought he saw a trace of that embarrassment in her eyes at the sight of him.

"Mason. We didn't expect you yet. I'll go and get Alexis." She rose as she spoke, but he held out his hand to deter her.

"I wanted to talk for a moment. I left the note at police headquarters yesterday, and Nikki Rivers called me back today."

Her color heightened a little at the mention of the note. "I suppose they couldn't make anything of it."

He shrugged. "She didn't say that, but the significant thing, to my mind, is that Penny is still wandering around town and no one has spotted her."

He could see the shiver that went through her at that. "She actually talked to Joseph. She could have—"

"Don't." His hand closed over hers. "Don't start imagining what might have happened. I'm the one she's after, not a child she's never seen before."

"The note sounded venomous toward me, as well." She seemed to force herself to meet his gaze. "I hope what she said didn't embarrass you."

"No, of course not." He had to do what he could to get things back on an easy basis between them. "That was just Penny striking out blindly. It's not worrying me, and I hope it's not upsetting you, either."

"It's not." The words were firm, but he didn't quite believe them. "It's just the idea of her hanging around, as you said."

He nodded. "I have to confess, I didn't sleep very well last night." He remembered that midnight waking.

"I got up at one point, thinking I heard something. Went to check on Alexis and found her bed empty. I nearly went ballistic."

"I can imagine." Her eyes were soft with sympathy.

"She came in from the bathroom, and I gave her such a hug…" He discovered that his voice had roughened. "Something happened. A first. She hugged me back. And I thought my heart would burst."

"You see. You're making progress with her. I knew you would."

"It scares me." He didn't mean to say that. The words just seemed to slip out of his mouth.

"Why?"

He shrugged. "What if I mess this up? What if she starts depending on me, and I let her down?"

"Why would you think that?" Exasperation filled her voice. "Mason, you're a responsible, caring person. Just because your parents didn't appreciate that, doesn't mean they were right. They weren't."

"I'm not so sure." He shook his head. "You don't know all of it, Jennifer. Maybe if you did, you wouldn't feel so sure about me."

"I can't imagine hearing anything that would make me respect you less."

"You don't know," he repeated stubbornly. He couldn't let go of it.

"Then tell me." She clasped his hand. "Just tell me, whatever it is."

He took a breath. He didn't talk about this, ever. But the urge to confide in her was overpowering.

"You know about how my brother died."

She nodded. "He was killed in an accident after a graduation party."

"That wasn't all of it." He stared at the bulletin board on the wall, but he wasn't seeing it. He was seeing himself, a skinny twelve-year-old, watching his brother get ready to go out.

"I knew, you see. I knew Gerry was going to that party. I knew he would binge drink, he always did. I tried to stop him, but I couldn't. I couldn't stop him, and I didn't want to tell, so I did nothing. And the next morning we learned that he was dead."

"Mason, I'm so sorry." Her eyes filled with tears. "But you can't think—"

"I didn't stop him. When my father looked at me over Gerry's casket and said he'd lost the wrong son, I knew he was right. It should have been me."

"No!" She clutched his hand so tightly that her nails dug into his skin. "You can't think that."

"It's true." It was almost a relief to tell someone. "Don't you get it? That's why I'm so scared to be Alexis's father. How can I forgive myself? How can God forgive me for all the people I've hurt, including poor little Josie?"

"Oh, Mason." The tears began to spill over. "Don't you see? You're still looking at it as if you're twelve and just lost your beloved older brother. This isn't about God not forgiving you. It's about you. If you can't forgive yourself, you're never going to be able to love anyone."

He shook his head. He'd like to believe that, but he couldn't.

"Listen to me." She held his hand between both of

hers. "God won't stop loving you. Even if you feel you're not worthy, God won't stop."

He wasn't sure he believed her, but something seemed to ease inside him at the words. "You know, you almost make me believe that's true."

"It is." Her gaze was filled with so much passion, so much love, that he felt himself swaying toward her.

He shouldn't even be thinking about this, let alone acting on the thought. But he reached out to touch her cheek, feeling the skin warm to his stroke.

His heart swelled. He caught her hands, drew her against him. "Jennifer." His voice was husky. "I want—"

His lips found hers, and all the arguments he was trying to make dissolved like mist in the sun. She was here. She was in his arms. Nothing else mattered.

That thought was a splash of cold water. Of course other things mattered. Alexis. Jennifer's feelings.

He drew back slowly. This wasn't fair. His feelings were in turmoil, and he and Jennifer were both trapped in a difficult situation. He had to keep all his concentration on protecting Alexis, and he suspected Jennifer would say the same.

He stroked her cheek again lightly, wanting to prolong the moment, to keep seeing the stars in her eyes.

"I guess—I guess maybe this isn't the right time for this."

She took a step back, a gentle smile curving her lips. "No, I guess it isn't."

"It will be. The police will clear all of this up, and then we'll be able to concentrate on our own lives."

"I pray so." Her voice was hardly more than a whisper.

"What I said about Gerry—you know, I've never told anyone all of that. I'm glad I told you."

"I'm glad you did, too. I want—"

"What?"

She shook her head. "It's nothing. There's just something I'd like to tell you one of these days, but now isn't the time. Alexis will be looking for you. We can talk later."

He nodded. "I'll hold you to that." He took a breath, realizing that his heart felt less constricted somehow. Jennifer was good for his daughter, and she was good for him, too.

FIFTEEN

Jennifer finished up the supply list and pushed back from the computer, stretching. She'd stayed late after everyone else had left, wanting to finish the paperwork that had been neglected since she'd spent so much time dealing with Alexis and Mason lately.

Mason. Just thinking his name brought that kiss back so vividly that her lips grew warm.

Maybe she'd better not think about that. Think instead about what he'd revealed to her about his brother. Her heart twisted. Poor Mason, blaming himself all these years. She knew, better than most people, how the words a child lived with could scar his life.

Now, maybe Mason had a chance to heal. His love for Alexis, growing stronger every day, would make him whole again.

She'd longed to tell him her own secret, but the time hadn't been right. Soon. Soon she'd tell him, and he'd know how much their friendship meant to her.

Friendship? No, that wasn't the word. She loved him. She wanted more than friendship. Maybe Mason did, too. Maybe, when this was all over...

She rose, heading for the supply room, the list in her hand. She should attend to what had to be done instead of longing for something that was out of her control. Perhaps the police would arrest Penny soon. That was something to cling to.

The hallway had grown shadowed while she was working. She was halfway down it when she heard the sound of the heavy fire door closing around the corner.

She turned, frowning. Who was coming into the building this late?

A footfall. Another. And then a figure came around the corner. Jennifer's heart seemed to stop. It was Penny, and she was carrying a gun.

Instinct took over from thought. She ducked into the nearest classroom, hearing Penny's steps, running now, running after her. She darted across the room to the other door, the one that led out into the opposite corridor. If she could get out there, maybe she could run for the stairs.

But Penny was already coming into the room, coming after her, the gun in her hand. She ducked behind the open door of a large metal storage cabinet, holding her breath. Maybe Penny would think she'd already gone out the far door. Then she could double back.

Penny's steps slowed. She was coming closer. She knew—she'd seen…

The steps stopped, only feet away, so close she could hear Penny's breath. Then a low laugh.

"Come out, come out, wherever you are." The voice was low and mocking.

For a moment she could do nothing but cringe back

against the wall, fear freezing her. She couldn't move, the gun…

No. She would not give in. Not like this.

Almost without thinking about it, she slid her hand behind the cabinet and then grasped the metal edge with the other.

"Come out," Penny snapped.

She took a breath, shoved as hard as she could, and prayed. The cabinet shivered, top-heavy. Then it began to move, toppling forward, gaining speed and crashed.

A shriek—metal? Penny? No waiting to see, just run for the door, back muscles tensing for a bullet.

It didn't come. Out into the hallway, and she hesitated. Which way to go?

Then she heard Penny coming and bolted blindly down the hall. *Please, Lord, please, Lord, be with me. Help me think.*

A phone. She had to get to a phone, or to an outside door. Those were her only chances. Go back toward her office?

But that would mean doubling back, and Penny was coming. Impossible. She ducked into the narrow passage that led through the custodian's room and into the gym.

Wait, no, not the gym. Those doors were locked at night with a chain, and she wouldn't have time to undo that. Penny's footfalls sounded behind her, a muttered curse…

She darted through the door that led into the cellars under the oldest part of the building, the area the teenagers called the catacombs.

It was dark, once the door banged behind her, but that

was good. Only a small amount of muted daylight filtered through the narrow windows that looked out onto window wells.

The cellars stretched around her, dirt floors, stone arches, dark shadows. Think. Quickly, decide before Penny came through the door.

There was another way out, she remembered seeing it once when the custodian had shown her around. A small, rickety stair leading up to a door that opened into the vestry. But where was it?

No time. She could hear the creak of the door behind her. She bolted into the shadows, holding her breath, feeling as if she'd never dare breathe again.

Run, don't stop thinking. Lord, guide me.

Where? Where was the door?

She ducked around another buttress and flattened herself against the wall, trying to catch her breath. They were playing hide and seek, but it was a dangerous game. She didn't have any illusions about Penny. Penny would use the gun if she had to.

No sound. Had Penny given up? Unlikely. She'd be waiting, hoping for Jennifer to make a sound and give herself away.

Her nerves stretched until it seemed they'd snap. She had to move, she had to. She couldn't be still any longer—

She heard a stealthy step. Penny, closer than she'd expected. Should she stay here, and pray she wouldn't find her? Run?

Suddenly the plan of the cellars came clear in her mind, and she knew where the little stairway was. Just down at the end of this wall, tucked into the corner.

Be brave. Take a chance. Don't stay here and wait to be trapped.

She took a cautious, silent step. Peered around the edge of the stone archway.

Penny was a shadow, not twelve feet away.

If she ran, Penny might fire the gun. If she didn't, Penny could round the corner and have her trapped.

Be with me, Father.

She dashed toward the end wall, heedless of the noise she made, hearing Penny behind her. Get there, get there, get up the stairs, bang the door behind her, find something to block it with. She'd be safe, she…

Her foot struck a loose stone. Her forward momentum sent her sprawling, the floor slamming into her so hard that she couldn't breathe, couldn't think.

And then she felt the cold muzzle of the gun against the back of her neck.

Penny muttered a few words she wouldn't care to repeat. "Get up." Penny kicked her, the blow landing in her ribs, sending pain through her. "Get up, or I'll take care of you right now."

She forced her muscles to work. *Push yourself to your feet. Don't give up. You can't give up. Think. There must be a way.*

The instant she was on her feet Penny shoved her face forward against the wall, thrusting the gun into her back.

"You're too much trouble. You and Mason both. The price has just doubled."

"Mason won't give you a cent." The bravado in her voice surprised her.

"Oh, I think he will." The gun pushed against her

harder. It would leave a bruise, not that that was going to matter. "You see, he's going to give me what I want, or I'll get to Alexis."

Fear tore at her throat. "You can't. You—"

"Yes. I can. Looks as if I'll have to show him I can get to the people he cares about anytime I like. I guess you're going to be the example for me." She chuckled. "Goodbye, Jennifer."

She was going to die. *Hold me, Lord—*

Pain exploded in the back of her head, and then there was only darkness.

Jennifer sat on the edge of the examining table, hands pressed against her temples. It had been hard enough to make her brain work to answer the questions the doctor had asked.

The police detectives had taken over the trauma room in the E.R., and their questions were even harder. If it weren't for Dad's stable presence next to her, she might have given in to the tears that pressed against her lids.

"Please—all these questions are wasting time." She had to make them understand, and she was afraid she sounded hysterical. "You have to be sure Alexis is safe. You have to!"

Dad's hand pressed on hers reassuringly. "I'm sure they've notified Mason." He gave Detective Paterson a challenging look. "If not, I'll go and call him right now myself."

Paterson's mouth tightened. "We've talked to Mr. Grant. He's aware of the situation. Now, Miss Pappas,

if you would just go over the sequence of events once
more—"

"I've already told you."

The tears grew a little harder to hold back, and that
was ridiculous. She was alive. She was all right except
for a mild concussion and a monstrous headache. Given
what she'd expected from Penny, she was fortunate.

*Thank You, Father. Thank You for being with me. I
was so afraid, but I knew You were there.*

"You were still pretty groggy the first time we
talked." Nikki Rivers sounded calm and reasonable, as
if the two of them were taking turns being nice. "Maybe
you'll think of something else if you go over it again."

She'd shake her head, but that would hurt too much.
Maybe if she went over it again, they'd leave her in
peace finally.

"Everyone else had left," she said with as much patience as she could muster. "I was just finishing when I
heard someone come through the fire door that's nearest
to the street. I looked, saw that it was Penny. She had a
gun in her hand, so I ran."

"You say you were able to identify the woman as Penny
Brighton. What was she wearing, do you remember?"

She frowned. "I just had a quick glimpse, and I was
too busy running to notice much. Dark pants, either a
dark shirt or jacket."

"Anything else?"

She closed her eyes, frowning with the effort of visu-
alizing. Then her eyes popped open again with startled
realization.

"Her hair. The last time I saw her it was red. Now it's dark brown."

"There, see? You did remember something else." Rivers sounded as if she were encouraging a child.

"Hair color's the easiest thing in the world to change." She rubbed her temple. "Are you sure Mason understood that Penny threatened Alexis?"

"Now, Miss Pappas—"

The exam-room door burst open and Mason barreled through. "Jennifer! Are you all right? What happened?" Ignoring the police, he came straight to her, nodding to her father.

Relief flooded through her at the sight of him. "I'm all right. But Alexis—where is she? Is she okay? You shouldn't have left her."

He clasped her hand. "She's safe. She's at Parker's house, and he and Kate are both with her. Nobody is going to get past Parker's security system."

She could breathe again, and a tear slid past her control. "That's good."

"Look here, are you sure she's all right?" Mason looked at Dad. "What did the doctor say?"

"She has a concussion. She ought to be home, resting, instead of answering questions." Dad glared at the detectives.

"Not just yet." Paterson loomed over her, and he didn't look as if he planned to go away soon. "You say that Penny Brighton chased you through the church cellars. That she caught up with you, threatened you with a gun. What exactly did she say?"

Jennifer gripped Mason's hand. "She said the price

had doubled. That Mason would pay unless he wanted something to happen to Alexis. That what happened to me would have to be an example to him."

Mason's fingers tightened on hers convulsively.

"What did you think she meant by that?" Paterson continued.

She fought to push the words out. "I thought she was going to kill me."

Mason made a small, choked sound. "You have to have protection. The woman's mad."

She let out a shaky breath. Oddly enough, having told the story a couple of times seemed to make thinking about it easier. "She's desperate, anyway, if not crazy."

"I'll pay her if that will end this."

"Now, Mr. Grant, you don't want to do that." Paterson seemed to try for calm. "Just let us handle this situation. That's our responsibility."

"You don't seem to be doing a great job so far. How can that woman be wandering around town without being caught?" Mason glared at him. "If it will protect my daughter and Miss Pappas from harm, I'll do whatever it takes."

Her heart warmed at being coupled with Alexis in his concern, but he was wrong to think a payoff would work.

"You can't, Mason. Don't you see? This has to end. You can't spend the rest of your life wondering if or when Penny's going to show up and threaten your daughter again."

"That's a good point," Nikki Rivers said quietly. "You could never be sure."

Mason looked rebellious for a moment, but then he nodded. "All right. We'll do it your way. But I'm not leaving my daughter until Penny Brighton is caught. And whether you're finished or not, it's time Miss Pappas went home. If you don't agree, maybe we can get the doctor in here for an opinion."

"That won't be necessary." Rivers stood, turned toward the door.

Jennifer sagged in relief. All she could think about was sliding into her bed and resting her aching head on the pillow.

Rivers took a step toward the door. Then she turned, zeroing in on Jennifer's face. "Just one more question for Miss Pappas."

She couldn't control the sigh that escaped. "What is it?"

Rivers raised an eyebrow. "It's a very simple one, really. Why didn't you tell us about your arrest record in Syracuse?"

The blow, coming from nowhere, nearly doubled her up. She couldn't breathe, couldn't think.

"Arrest record?" Mason's tone was incredulous. "That's ridiculous."

"Miss Pappas was arrested in Syracuse, New York, eighteen months ago, for interfering in the custody of a minor child." Paterson said the words distinctly, as if to forestall argument.

Mason—she'd wanted to tell him, but she couldn't. Now she couldn't even look at him.

"My daughter was cleared." Her father spoke for her, and she heard the suppressed fury in his voice. "She did nothing wrong."

"She was arrested and charged," Rivers said, her voice mild. "And in a case involving the custody of a child. Sort of coincidental that she's involved in something similar again, isn't it?"

"That's a ridiculous assumption." Dad stood, taking a protective step closer to her and resting a comforting hand on her shoulder. "Jennifer's profession involves her with children every day. The police were completely wrong in that situation in Syracuse. They admitted that. She was innocent."

"That right, Miss Pappas?" Paterson's tone demanded an answer.

Jennifer forced herself to look up. "That's right."

"Then why did you leave? Why come here? And why doesn't anyone here in Magnolia Falls seem to know about it if you're so innocent?"

The barrage of questions stunned her, but she couldn't afford to react that way. She couldn't be numb, or hurt, because the more time the police wasted on looking into her past, the less likely they were to concentrate on finding Penny.

She looked straight at the questioner. "It's a sad fact that the innocent suffer when they're accused of a crime, even when they're cleared. The announcement of my arrest put the day-care center's name in headlines. The report that I'd been cleared rated a small paragraph on a back page. I didn't want to cause the center any more harm, so I resigned."

She couldn't look at Mason, not yet. But he wasn't holding her hand any longer. Her heart seemed to crack just a little.

"And you told no one here about it," Paterson said. "That seems odd, for an innocent person."

Dad had urged her all along to confide in her friends, and she hadn't been able to bring herself to do it. Now she was going to pay the penalty.

"I have a right to my privacy." It sounded feeble, even to her. "My past has nothing to do with what's happening now. It's not important. Protecting Alexis, that's what's important." She struggled to look at Mason. "You understand, don't you?"

"Yes. I understand." He said the right words.

But she saw the doubt in his eyes. The disappointment. And she knew then.

Whatever might have been between them was gone now. It would never be.

She hadn't trusted his friendship enough to be honest with him, and now she wasn't even going to have that.

SIXTEEN

"But why can't I go to after-school?" Alexis hadn't made any objection to staying home from school the next day, but she obviously felt differently about the after-school program.

"I'd just prefer that you stay home today." *Because I can't bear to have you out of my sight,* Mason thought, but he didn't want to frighten her.

This was the first time Alexis had argued with him about anything. That probably meant she felt more comfortable with him, but he'd rather she hadn't picked this moment to start.

"Please, Alexis, just go along with me on this. How about if we order a pizza for supper?"

She ignored his attempt at distraction. "Can I go tomorrow?"

"I don't know." He resorted to the parent's last refuge. "We'll see."

How long would it take for the police to catch up with Penny? After the attack on Jennifer, he didn't want Alexis out of his sight. Penny was violent and unpredictable, and he was beginning to fear she'd elude the police indefinitely. How would they live then?

"If we get pizza, can Jennifer come over and have supper with us?" Alexis shifted gears, but this was not a welcome subject, either.

"Jennifer's probably busy. Maybe she can come another time."

Alexis's eyes filled with tears. "Doesn't Jennifer like me anymore?"

The tears stabbed him to the heart, and he put his arm cautiously around Alexis's shoulders. She still seemed shy of any expressions of affection, and he didn't want to push her.

"Sugar, of course Jennifer still likes you. It's just that she— Well, she had an accident, a bump on the head yesterday. That's why I went down to the hospital, and you went to Parker's house to play with Brandon. She probably still doesn't feel too well. I imagine she'll want to rest after work today."

"How did she bump her head?" Alexis was nothing if not persistent. Usually he admired that quality, but in this case…

"She fell," he said shortly. *She fell because Penny crashed a gun into the back of her head and could have killed her. And if she had, that would be my responsibility.*

He shook off that thought before it could paralyze him. He gave his daughter a quick hug. "Why don't you go e-mail some of your friends and ask them to let you know what you missed in school today? Maybe you can get started on your homework."

She stared at him for a moment, as if she knew he

was hiding something. Then, to his relief, she nodded and headed for the stairs.

He walked over to the living-room window that over-looked the marsh and stared out at the rain that had been pelting down most of the day. The same fears kept pounding at him, as relentless as the rain.

Jennifer. Each time he thought of her facing Penny alone, the burden of guilt became nearly unbearable.

Because of Jennifer's involvement with him, she could have been killed. Because of him, she'd had to bear that police suspicion, the humiliation of having her past troubles dragged out to cause her more grief.

He ran his hand through his hair and gripped the back of his neck, where the tension seemed to be taking up permanent residence. That revelation had stunned him for a moment, but whatever had happened at that day-care center in Syracuse, he knew Jennifer well enough to know she'd never have done anything to harm a child. And the situation had obviously caused her a great deal of pain.

Why hadn't she told him? That was a separate hurt from the rest of his anxiety. He'd talked to her about things he'd never told anyone else. Why hadn't she trusted him with the truth?

He leaned his forehead against the windowpane. He'd spent the past ten years avoiding getting close to anyone. He'd told himself that way he couldn't hurt anybody. He could cope.

Now— Well, if he cut off his relationship with Jennifer, it might keep her safe, even though it would be like cutting off his arm. And even then, it might not.

Penny was incalculable. If she'd decided she wanted to get even with Jennifer for her interference—

He couldn't let himself believe that. This was between him and Penny. And Alexis. His heart clenched. He'd never imagined loving anyone the way he loved his child. He had to protect Alexis.

He'd tried to run from caring for anyone, but God had backed him into a corner, forcing him to face what he feared most, forcing him to care.

Trying to hold back tears, he put his hands over his face.

Can you forgive me, Lord? I've let down so many people. I can't do that to Alexis. Or Jennifer. I need help. Please, help me.

Jennifer checked on activities in the gym and then went slowly back toward the arts-and-crafts room. She had to pass the door that led into the cellars, but she tried not to look at it. She couldn't shake the feeling that Penny was there, somewhere, hiding and ready to pounce out at her if she relaxed.

Father, You have been here for me through everything. Please, hold my hand. Help me to stop giving in to these foolish, imaginary fears. The real things are enough to face.

She wasn't even sure how to pray about her personal crisis. It was her fault in many ways. If she had been open about her past when she came to Magnolia Falls, even if she had told her circle of friends once they'd become close again, her arrest would be old news by now.

Instead—well, how long before her secret got around

town? How long before her friends started looking at her askance? How long before she'd have to resign?

The pastor would stand up for her, of course. He'd already stopped by to express his concern and support. But it wouldn't be fair to let the program suffer because of her.

As for Mason… She paused in the hallway, listening to the chatter of the children in the art room. Well, she'd already seen Mason's reaction, hadn't she? His withdrawal in the trauma room had been evident to her, if it hadn't been to anyone else.

He'd called the house, last night, and stayed on the phone just long enough to ask her father how she was. He hadn't asked to talk to her, and he hadn't brought Alexis to the after-school program. That spoke volumes, didn't it? He didn't trust her with his child.

The fire door at the end of the hall swung open, and she tensed, ready to flee, images of Penny with a gun flooding her mind. But it was Mason who came around the corner, not Penny.

He rushed toward her, his face ashen. "Alexis—have you seen her?"

Her heart nearly stopped at the question. "No. You didn't— I thought she wasn't coming today. What's happened?"

"I hoped she might be here." He ran his hand through his hair. "She wanted to come, but I felt as if I had to keep her in sight today. Now look what's happened."

She put her hand on his arm. "Mason, stop. You're not making any sense. Tell me what's going on."

He took a breath, trying to compose himself, but she could feel the fear that drove him.

"She was— I thought she was in her room on the computer. But when I went up to check on her, she was gone."

"You checked the house."

"Of course." He moved impatiently. "The alarm system had been turned off from the inside. It looks as if she just walked out the back door."

"Were any of her things missing?"

She had to stay calm, keep him calm, so they could figure this out. Why on earth would Alexis walk away? She'd certainly shown that she was afraid of Penny.

"Just her jacket." He yanked out his cell phone. "I have to alert the police. I hoped she was here. She wanted to be. Wanted to see you."

And he hadn't let her. She pushed away the hurt. "I'm going to get Brandon. He's the one she talks to. Maybe he has some idea of where she'd go."

She hurried into the art room, leaving Mason talking on the cell phone. Brandon, looking a little startled at being summoned, followed her out, and she led him and Mason into her office.

Sitting down, she drew Brandon close to her knees, trying to ease his apprehension. "Brandon, you remember Alexis's father, don't you?"

He nodded, eyes wide.

She hesitated to say the rest of it, but if they wanted the child's help, they'd have to be honest. "Alexis left the house this afternoon without telling her dad. We don't know where she is. Do you have any ideas about what's going on with her? Did she tell you about anything that was worrying her?"

He shook his head, clasping his hands behind his back, and she knew instantly that he was hiding something.

"Please listen, Brandon. Alexis could be in trouble. In danger. If you have any clue about what's happened to her, you have to tell us."

The boy's forehead furrowed. "But what if—what if I promised not to say anything?"

Her heart leaped. He did know something.

"Brandon—" she began, but Mason knelt beside him, pre-empting her.

"Listen, Brandon." She could imagine how much effort it took to keep his voice even. "I know how you feel. One time I promised my brother I wouldn't tell about something he was doing. So I didn't. But then he—he got hurt, and I felt as if it was my fault. Do you understand what I'm saying?"

Brandon nodded slowly. "I guess that maybe you have to break a promise if it means keeping someone from being hurt."

"Exactly. So if you know where my daughter would go, you have to tell us, so we can keep her safe."

"Not that," Brandon said. "I don't know that. It's just that she was talking about that woman, the one the police are after."

"Penny," Jennifer said. As much as all of the adults had talked about the situation with Penny lately, Brandon was bound to know something.

He nodded. "Alexis said that she had an e-mail from her. It made her scared."

"An e-mail! Are you sure?" Mason exchanged looks with Jennifer. "How would Penny get her e-mail address?"

He shrugged. "I dunno. But that's what she said. She didn't want to tell me, but I could see something was wrong, so I bugged her, and she told me."

"Did she say what Penny wanted?" Mason kept his voice calm, but there was a white line around his lips.

"No." Brandon shook his head violently. "Just that it made her scared. I told her she oughta tell you."

"That was good advice," Jennifer said. "Did she say why she didn't tell her daddy?"

Brandon shrugged. "I guess." He looked reluctant.

"Please tell me. You won't hurt my feelings." Mason was reading the child well.

"I guess she said about how you didn't know her very long. That maybe, if she was too much trouble, you wouldn't want to keep her."

That had to be a blow to Mason's heart, but he managed to keep his face calm. "I promise you, I would keep her no matter what. She's my daughter. Do you have any idea where she might go?"

Brandon shook his head. "I'd tell you if I did. Honest I would."

"Thank you, Brandon. You've really helped." Mason rose, looking at her. "I'm going back to the house to check the computer."

"I'll go with you." She stood, taking Brandon's hand. "Just let me take Brandon back to his class and ask the art teacher to take over for me."

Without waiting for an argument, she hurried out of the room. Whether Mason wanted her or not, whether he trusted her or not, she wasn't going to be left out of this, not when Alexis might need her.

* * *

"Alexis! Are you here?" Mason had barely thrown the door of his house open when he was calling his daughter's name.

No answer. Just silence.

He started for the stairs, but Jennifer caught his arm. "What about the answering machine? She might have called you."

He nodded, detouring to the phone that stood on the counter. A quick glance, and he was shaking his head. "Nothing. Let's see about the computer."

She followed him up the stairs, trying to think this through calmly. They wouldn't help Alexis by running off in all directions.

"What did the police say?" Little though she wanted to see them again, they had to be involved in this.

"The detectives are meeting me here." Mason threw the words over his shoulder as he rushed into his daughter's room.

The new computer sat innocently on the small white desk Mason had bought to hold it for his daughter. It hurt to think that Mason's gift was being used against him.

Mason switched the computer on and tapped his fingers impatiently while it booted up. As soon as it had, he connected to the Internet and went to the e-mail program.

"If she deleted the message, this is going to be harder, but maybe it's still here." He twitched impatiently, waiting for the program to appear. "I still don't see how Penny could have gotten Alexis's e-mail address."

"Alexis probably gave it out to all her friends at school. And it may be on the class Web page, as well.

As daring as Penny is, she could have spun some story to one of the children to get it."

"Daring?" he repeated. "Reckless is more like it. Maybe that's why the police haven't been able to catch up with her. They're acting as if she's some rational criminal, but she's far from that."

"Yes." How did you categorize a woman who had apparently killed her friend to steal a baby? Who seemed to have no conscience at all?

"Here's the inbox." Mason went quickly down through the e-mails. It looked as if Alexis had saved all of them. "There." He clicked, and a message appeared.

He doesn't really want you. He only took you because he had to. It's time you were back with me. Leave the house and don't let him know where you're going. Quickly! I'll be waiting in my car around the corner, in front of the red house. Don't keep me waiting long. And don't tell him. If you do, I'll know. I'll go straight to the church and I'll hurt your friend Jennifer.

Jennifer's breath caught. Penny had used a threat to her to force Alexis to do what she wanted.

"That poor child. Reading this—"

"She did what Penny said," he finished for her. He glanced at his watch. "They've had a long start. How we're going to find them—"

"Penny will be in touch with you. After all, that's what this is all about, isn't it? She wants money from you, and she's using Alexis to get it."

"You're right." He ran his hand through his hair in

frustration. "Of course she'll be in touch. I wonder—"
He clicked the button to check mail.

A chill settled over her when she saw an e-mail come
in with Mason's name in caps in the subject line. He
clicked open the file and read aloud.

I have the kid. Bring the money to Magnolia Falls
State Park at sunset. Bring Jennifer to carry it to me.
No police. I'll call your cell phone to tell you where
to meet me.

Mason shut the file, swung away from the desk and
headed for the door.

"Wait. What are you doing? The police—"

"You heard what she said." Mason's face was tor-
mented. "I've done everything the cops told me, and this
is the result. Now I'm going to pay her off."

"Mason—" But he was already starting down the
steps, and she had to run to catch up with him. "At least
tell the police what you're doing."

"No." He spared a distracted glance for her. "Go
home, Jennifer. I'll call you."

"No." Much as her insides quaked at the thought of
confronting Penny again, she couldn't let him go alone.
"She said to bring me."

He shrugged impatiently. "If you're not there, she'll
have to deal with me." He headed out the door, and she
followed him.

"Either take me, or I call the police right now and tell
them what you're doing."

He glared at her, and she returned it with as stubborn a look as she could muster.

"All right." He capitulated so suddenly it took her by surprise. "Get in." He yanked the car door open. "Hurry up. I want to get out of here before the police get here."

Breathing a silent prayer, Jennifer slid into the car.

SEVENTEEN

Jennifer found herself hoping the police would come screaming down the block before they got away from the house, but it didn't happen. Mason's hands clenched the steering wheel as he drove down the quiet street. She could sense his desire to speed, but he controlled himself with what had to be enormous effort.

Mason turned toward the center of town, instead of in the direction of the highway.

"Where are we going?" She clutched the armrest when he took a turn a little too abruptly.

"The office. I don't keep that kind of money at home."

"I wouldn't expect you to have it at the office, either."

His mouth tightened. "I kept the original payment she demanded in the office safe. I've added to it. Just in case."

"It was always in your mind that you'd pay her off." She couldn't say she was surprised. Mason would do whatever he thought necessary to keep Alexis safe. "But—"

"I know what you're going to say." His voice was sharp. "I even agree. Paying her off won't end it. But she's got Alexis, so she's calling the shots."

"I know." Fear tightened her throat. "I know."

She didn't speak again while he pulled into a lot behind the store, got out and ran toward the back door. Instead, hands clasped in her lap, she prayed, the pleas pouring out in a torrent of emotion.

She loved that child. She loved Mason. Even if she had to say goodbye to them when this was all over, she'd never stop loving them.

Mason was back in moments, carrying a small navy duffel bag that he tossed casually into the backseat.

"That's it?" It was hard for her even to imagine that amount of money in one small bag.

He nodded. "Nothing from the police. I thought they might have called here."

She hadn't thought of that. "They have your cell number. When they find you're not at the house, they'll call that."

"I know." He pulled out onto the street and headed west, toward the state park which lay a good half-hour's drive from town. "I can't turn it off, because Penny might call."

"What are you going to say to the police?" Somehow it was easier to go on talking about details and logistics. It kept her from thinking about things that hurt too much.

"Just what I told you." His tone was harsh and uncompromising. "Right or wrong, I'll pay Penny off to get my daughter back. Once she's safe, I'll tell the police where we are." He shot a sideways glance at her. "Not going to argue?"

"No. You're right. Penny has Alexis, so we have to

do what she says." But she didn't think the police were going to see it that way.

The cell phone rang just as they cleared the town limits. She could only hear Mason's end of the conversation, of course, but she could guess what Paterson and/or Rivers was saying.

Mason's expression never changed. He reiterated his plan twice. Then he hung up.

"Did they agree?"

"No. But this time they don't have a choice." His mouth clamped shut on the words.

Her heart clenched. "She's going to be all right. We'll get her back. I've been praying constantly, and I know God will keep her safe."

"I've been praying, too." His lips twisted. "It seems there's nothing like fatherhood to make a man see that he needs God."

One good thing had come out of this terrible time, at any rate. "I know He's listening." It was all she could manage without letting tears show in her voice. Maybe it was enough.

The miles ticked by. Mason glanced often at the cell phone he'd put on the console between the seats, as if willing it to ring.

Alexis, we're coming for you. It's going to be all right. She thought the words, as if somehow God might send the message to Alexis's heart.

After a long silence, Mason cleared his throat. "There's something I want to say to you."

A chill settled into her bones. "If it's about what the police said yesterday—"

"Not exactly." He shook his head abruptly. "It was ridiculous, their thinking you were involved with Penny. Or imagining that you'd ever be guilty of anything that would harm a child. I know you better than that."

"But I didn't tell you about it." Her voice thickened with tears. "I'm sorry. I wanted to. I started to tell you, a couple of times."

"Tell me now."

"Now?"

He nodded. "We're still fifteen minutes from the park. Stop putting it off, wondering if it's the right time. Just say it."

Maybe he was right. Maybe she had worried too much about finding the right moment. She took a breath. This was going to be hard.

"You heard what the detectives said. It was a custody situation. We knew, at the day care, that the little boy, Justin, was never to be turned over to anyone but his mother."

She closed her eyes for a moment. This was the humiliating part. "I met someone—he stopped to help me when I found my tire was flat. He seemed nice. Asked me out for coffee. Then to dinner. I hadn't been dating anyone. I guess I was flattered. He even came to the house and met my dad."

"It was the child's father," Mason said.

She nodded. "Looking back it seems so obvious, but at the time— Well, why would I make any connection?"

"You wouldn't," he said quickly, and she was grateful.

"He made arrangements to pick me up at the center one day to take me to lunch. When he arrived, the receptionist buzzed him in, directed him to my office. As soon as he was out of her sight, he doubled back and went to the play-yard. He grabbed Justin and tried to run for it."

Her voice was shaking, so she stopped and took a breath. "Luckily a few arriving parents heard the outcry and managed to stop him before he got away."

"That was fortunate."

"It was a godsend." She breathed the words like a prayer. "The aftermath— Well, you already know some of that. The mother accused me of being part of it, I was arrested, charged…" The nightmare still shook her.

"I'm sorry." He reached across to clasp her hand for a moment. "Sorry you had to go through that. And sorry you didn't feel you could tell me sooner."

"I've been a hypocrite." She had to force the words out. "I keep saying that I trust God, but I haven't trusted the people He brought into my life." A tear escaped, and she wiped it away impatiently. "None of that matters now. The only thing that's important is getting Alexis back."

"Yes." His voice went tight. "There's the park entrance. Penny should be calling soon."

Maybe, in some small corner of her heart, she hoped for a word of forgiveness from Mason. But what she'd said was the truth. The only thing that mattered now was getting Alexis back.

Her fingers tightened on the armrest as they turned into the park entrance. Nothing else was important.

Mason drove into the main parking lot, not sure where else to go. He stared at the cell phone, willing it to ring.

Jennifer touched his arm, and he was so tense he

jerked away from her hand. "She may be watching, waiting to be sure we didn't bring the police."

He nodded. He ought to say something, talk to her, but every fiber of his being was concentrated on Alexis. He was so close now—he could almost sense her presence. Surely she could feel him worrying about her, willing her to be safe.

Jennifer leaned forward, looking out at the parking lot, her face averted. "It looks as if the park is nearly empty at this hour on a weekday. Penny must have known that."

He nodded again. Alexis, where are you? *Lord, please keep her safe. She's an innocent child. She doesn't deserve to suffer this way.*

The rain had slacked off to a gray drizzle. It cut down the visibility. Would that work to Penny's advantage, or to his?

He didn't have any illusions about Penny. She was perfectly capable of trying to get away with both Alexis and the money. Every fiber of his body grew tense at the thought.

That was not going to happen. No matter what the cost, he would get Alexis away from Penny.

The shrilling of the cell phone, when it finally came, shattered the silence. He sensed Jennifer's wince as he grabbed the phone.

"Don't talk. Just listen." Penny didn't sound mocking now—just cold and deadly. "Both of you get out of the car with the money. Start walking down the trail to Magnolia Pond. Take the cell phone."

The connection was broken before he could argue. He

slid out of the car, reaching into the back to grab the bag with the money. When Jennifer got out, he shook his head.

"Don't bother." She sounded as determined in her way as Penny had been. "I'm coming. Which way?"

He nodded toward the trail entrance. "Toward the pond." He tucked the cell phone into his shirt pocket and led the way.

Jennifer turned up the collar of her Windbreaker against the drizzle. She glanced back at the parking lot as they entered the path. "You don't think the police will interfere, do you?"

"I don't see how they can. They don't know the meeting place." He'd call them afterward, once he had his daughter safe.

They walked down the trail, wet pine needles squishing underfoot. There was no sound—not an animal rustling through the woods, not a bird singing. Only the drip of water on thirsty plants accompanied them.

He glanced at Jennifer's face. She was praying, he realized. Her eyes focused inward, and now and then her lips moved slightly.

Hear our prayers, Lord. Keep Alexis safe.

If they all came out of this in one piece…

It hit him, then. He hadn't made arrangements for Alexis if anything happened to him. He hadn't changed his will or appointed a guardian.

Too late. It seemed he was always trying to do the right thing too late. There was one thing he could do, though.

He turned to Jennifer, grasping her arm. "Before we go on, I have to ask you something. If anything happens to me, will you make sure Alexis is taken care of?"

Her face went even paler, if that was possible. "Nothing is going to happen to you."

"If. If it does. Promise me, please."

"I promise." She whispered the words, and her lips trembled.

"Good." It wasn't enough, but it would have to do. Alexis was his daughter, so she'd inherit, even without a will. And she'd have Jennifer and her grandparents and her aunt to see that she was all right.

Jennifer stepped on a branch that snapped off loudly, and she seemed to shiver. "We must be almost to the pond. I hope this isn't some sort of elaborate ploy to find out if we're being followed."

"If it is, she should be satisfied by now."

But he was beginning to wonder. Where was Penny? He'd expected her to show herself by now.

Another dreary, wet hundred feet, and they stepped out of the woods and into the cleared area by the pond. There was a picnic shelter ahead of them. A flicker of movement had him stiffening, and then Penny stepped out of the shelter. She had a gun in her right hand. With the left, she grasped Alexis by the arm.

He looked at his daughter, and his heart seemed to snap. Her small face was rigid, her expression so withdrawn it almost seemed she wasn't even there.

EIGHTEEN

Jennifer sensed Mason make an abrupt move toward his daughter, and she grabbed his arm. The gun—

Fast as a snake striking, Penny moved the gun so that it pointed at the back of Alexis's neck. Jennifer's breath caught in a spasm of fear, but the child's stoic expression didn't change.

"Don't," she said softly to Mason.

His jaw was rigid. "I won't."

"That's right," Penny said. She wiggled the gun. "Just move out away from the trees a little more, so I can see you."

They obeyed. What else could they do? Surely Mason realized that as well as she did. Penny had Alexis and Penny had the gun, so she was the boss.

"That's enough." The words were sharp, and for the first time she realized Penny was afraid. Or if not afraid, at least nervous. Being on the run must have eroded some of her confidence. "Mason, you stay where you are. Hand the bag to Jennifer."

She reached for it, but Mason suddenly pulled back.

His voice was loud. "I'll bring you the money. Leave Jennifer out of it."

"Not a chance." Penny's lips twitched in a parody of a smile. "Jennifer's in it to the neck. Now, you stay there, nice and quiet, if you want the kid in one piece. And Jennifer brings me the money."

Quickly, before Mason could react, before her courage could fail, Jennifer grabbed the bag from him.

"All right. I'm coming. We're doing exactly as you say." She called the words to Penny, but they were meant for Mason, too. He understood, didn't he? They didn't have a choice.

Jennifer walked toward Penny slowly, holding the bag in her right hand, her left open and away from her body to show that it was empty. Not that Penny would expect her to try anything, in any event.

Penny thought of her as a mouse. That was why she wanted her to carry the bag. She didn't want to give Mason an excuse to get close enough to try anything.

Her foot hit a patch of gravel, and she stumbled a step before regaining her balance. She shot a look at Penny. The gun was still pointed at Alexis, and the lack of expression on the child's face cut her to the heart.

"You don't need to point that thing at Alexis. We're doing just what you say."

"Shut up." Penny's nerves seemed to be growing ragged. That gave her a little extra courage.

"Look, here's the money." She held the bag out enticingly. "Just take it and let Alexis go. You can keep the gun on me until you're safe."

"Stop telling me what to do." The gun wavered a little, as if Penny wasn't sure which way to point it.

She had a problem, Jennifer realized. She had the gun in one hand and held Alexis with the other. She'd have to relinquish one or the other to take the bag.

"Here's the money." She was only a few feet away now. "Let Alexis go to her father."

Penny bared her teeth. "No way." She nodded toward the ground. "Just put the bag at my feet. Then I'll tell you what to do next."

"Please, Penny—"

"Do it!"

She tried to catch Alexis's gaze, to give her a reassuring look, but Alexis seemed to be beyond that. It was almost as if she'd stopped seeing or hearing anything.

She bent slowly and put the bag on the ground in front of Penny. She started to straighten, caught a flash of movement as Penny raised her arm, and then swung it down fiercely.

An instinctive reaction had her flinching away just as the blow landed, so that it hit the side of her head rather than her temple. It was still heavy enough to send her sprawling to the ground, the wind knocked out of her when she landed.

She rolled, groaning, trying to focus her gaze. She sensed Mason move, but Penny stopped him with a gesture of gun.

Jennifer pushed herself up to her elbow. Penny had the gun pointed at Mason now, and with a shiver of fear she understood. This was where Penny had been headed all along.

Mason held out his hands, palms out. "Easy, Penny. Just let Alexis go. You have the money. No one will try to stop you."

"Money!" Her voice dripped with venom. "Do you really think this was just about the money? When I've been suffering from other people's betrayals for years?"

"Penny—"

She silenced him with a motion of the gun. "That stupid Josie. She promised me the baby. It was so easy. We went up to New England, went to a hospital where nobody knew us and just switched names. As far as anyone knew, it was Penny Kessler who had the baby. I had to have a baby, don't you see? I had to persuade the Kessler family that I'd had Adam's baby, so I could inherit."

"We see." Mason took a cautious step toward Penny. "But something went wrong."

"Josie." She spat out the name. "We got all the way back to Magnolia Falls with that brat squalling in the backseat, and Josie tried to back out. Said she'd go to her family, get them to help her keep the baby. I couldn't let her do that."

"So you persuaded her to go on campus with you, knowing everyone had left for break." Mason took another step under cover of his words.

Jennifer knew what he was trying to do. He wanted to get close enough to rush Penny if she tried to leave with Alexis. She had to get herself together so that she could help him.

She struggled to get both hands planted on the ground and her knees under her so that she could move when he did.

"It wasn't hard to get her on campus. I just told her you were waiting for her." Penny sounded proud of herself. "That construction at the library was perfect. I hit her, shoved her into the trench. The workmen covered her up, and no one was the wiser."

"But it didn't work," Mason pointed out.

Penny's face twisted. "Those self-righteous Kesslers wouldn't accept the baby as Adam's without a blood test. So I had nothing but what I could get out of my parents and the father of the baby I lost."

Jennifer pressed her fingers to her aching head for a moment. So Penny really had been pregnant at one time—

"Cornell Rutherford." Mason supplied the name as if he were sure.

Somehow she wasn't surprised when Penny nodded. "Cornell was useful to me in a lot of ways, until he was stupid enough to get involved with that gambling scam and get caught. Then I had to do it on my own. I always had to do everything on my own!"

Penny was losing it. Jennifer fought to make her limbs obey her, pushing herself upright, but it was like swimming through molasses, and Penny—Penny was aiming the gun at Mason, shaking with fury, she was going to shoot. Jennifer would never get to her in time.

"No!" Alexis suddenly came alive, shrieking at the top of her lungs. "No! You can't hurt my daddy!" She struggled, striking out at Penny, heedless of the gun, of the danger.

Terror sent new strength surging through Jennifer. She lunged toward the two figures. She had to get between Alexis and that gun, she had to—

She staggered into them, grabbing for the gun, but Penny pulled it free, she was aiming it…

Mason barreled into them, knocking all of them to the ground. Jennifer felt Alexis's slight form, grabbed her and rolled free of them, sheltering Alexis with her body, waiting for a shot to ring out.

Instead she heard shouts, voices, the wail of sirens. Powerful lights stabbed through the gloom of the pavilion, outlining Mason and Penny. He had hold of the hand with the gun. He was forcing it down, away from them.

And then the police rushed from the woods and grabbed Penny, and it was over.

Jennifer's heart felt as if it would burst as she watched Mason, sitting on a bench in the pavilion, cuddle his daughter close to him. Alexis held on to him as if she'd never let go.

"It's all right now, sugar." Mason stroked her hair. "You're safe. We never have to worry about her again."

"Daddy," Alexis murmured. It was all she seemed to want to say.

A tear spilled over, and Jennifer wiped it away. *Thank You, Father. Thank You for bringing us safely through this trial, and for bringing Mason and his daughter together.*

If there was nothing else for her, that was enough.

Penny had been taken away in a police car, still shouting her anger and hatred for everyone she felt had wronged her. It would be nice to think they'd never have to see her again, but there would be a trial. There would be newspaper publicity. They weren't finished with all of this yet, but at least the danger was past.

"I don't understand." Mason glanced at Nikki Rivers, who was waiting patiently to talk with him. Paterson had gone to the station with the prisoner. "How did you know where to find us?"

"You should have told us, you know." Rivers gave him a reproving look. "But I guess I can understand why you didn't. We were able to trace your location through the cell phone, so we knew in general where you were headed. Your car was spotted, and we followed at what we hoped was a safe distance."

"I have to admit, I was glad to see you."

She shrugged. "Looked as if the three of you had the situation in hand by the time we reached you. You make a good team."

Mason nodded, holding his daughter closer. But he didn't look at Jennifer, and she suddenly felt chilled and exhausted.

"Are you going to be able to nail her for everything she's done?" Mason avoided saying Penny's name.

"For the original crime and for the abduction of your daughter, certainly. I'm not sure we'll ever know the full extent of her crimes, unless either she or Rutherford decides to spill." She shrugged. "Stranger things have happened. I'm sure the District Attorney will push them on it."

"There's no question of bail, I hope."

"I think you can be sure of that." Rivers's gaze touched the child. "Why don't you take your daughter home, Mr. Grant? I'll need to talk with her, I'm afraid, but that can wait until tomorrow." She smiled, her usual all-business expression dissolving into warmth, and suddenly she was a sympathetic human being instead of a tough cop. "I'm glad this turned out all right."

He nodded. "So are we."

Rivers walked off, consulting with one of the uniformed officers. Mason's car had been brought from the other lot by the police and stood waiting.

Jennifer pushed herself away from the pavilion post that had been supporting her. "I can ask one of the officers to drive me, so you can go straight home."

Better that way, to give Mason and Alexis this time together. They needed each other, not her.

But the look Mason turned on her was astonished. "Why would we do that?" He held out his hand to her. "And why are you standing way over there?"

"I thought— I wanted to give you and Alexis some privacy."

He smiled, the tension easing out of his face. "We don't need privacy. We need you. Don't we, sugar?"

Alexis looked up. Then she held out her hand, too.

It only took a few steps until she was next to them. Mason pulled her down on the bench and drew her close. Alexis grabbed her hand and held on tightly.

"We're not moving from this spot until I tell both of you something." Mason's deep voice roughened. "I love you. Both of you. So much. God must have forgiven me for all the things I've done wrong if He was willing to bring you both into my life. Okay?"

Jennifer nodded, her eyes filling with tears. Mason understood, finally. He'd been willing to sacrifice his life for her and for Alexis. He wasn't going to let them down—not now, not ever.

She put her arms around both of them. *Thank You, Lord. Thank You.*

EPILOGUE

The sunlight filtered through the live oaks on the Magnolia College campus, and Jennifer fanned herself with the program for the dedication of the new library wing. The ceremony had been brief, and now people gathered in small groups under the gracious old trees, talking, laughing, reminiscing.

She stood in a loose circle of the college friends who'd all played a role, one way or another, in bringing the truth about Josie to light.

Mason handed her a glass of sweet tea. "Do you know where Alexis is?"

Even months later, he was still a little overprotective where his daughter was concerned. Actually, Alexis seemed to enjoy it.

"Right over there." She nodded toward the refreshment table. "She and Brandon have been filching cookies. I guess they need the sugar for energy after all the running around they've been doing."

"How they can do that in this heat, I can't imagine," Kate said, as she and Parker joined the group. "It was a nice ceremony wasn't it?"

"Short," Parker said. "That's the best kind of ceremony." He smiled at his wife, as if remembering their wedding.

Mason grinned. "I thought Steff and Dee did a great job of stressing the positive aspects of the new wing to the press, without mentioning anything about discovering a body."

"That's our job," Dee pointed out, her fiancé, Edgar Ortiz, nodding his agreement.

"Thanks for the kind words." Steff looked elegant, as always, in a cream suit had hid the small bulge of her pregnancy, but the way her husband, Trevor, hovered over her would have given their secret away even if she hadn't told them.

"If Josie's body hadn't been found when we started construction, a lot of things would be different." Trevor's crew had made that gruesome find, so he was hardly likely to forget it.

"Poor Josie." Kate's sympathy brought tears to her eyes. "She didn't deserve what happened to her."

Jennifer felt Mason move slightly, and she could only hope he wasn't blaming himself again.

"I've been talking to Josie's sister about having a memorial service for her in a month or two," he said. "I thought we might all like to have a chance to say goodbye."

People nodded, and Jennifer's heart swelled with pride. Trust Mason to think of something like that. Now that he was out from under the shadow of his family's expectations, he felt free to express his kind heart.

"Maybe after the trial would be best." Dee, ever the public relations expert, pointed out. "We don't want the newspaper reporters to decide that should be part of their coverage."

"I just hope Penny gets everything that's coming to her. She hurt so many people." Cassie was uncharacteristically severe.

"I don't suppose we'll ever know the truth about my brother's death." Steff's thoughts returned, as always, to her brother Adam. "She and Rutherford are still busy blaming each other, I understand."

"Let the D.A. sort it out," Trevor said soothingly. "It'll be okay. She's going to pay the penalty, in any event."

"We'll all be okay." People looked at her, and Jennifer realized she'd spoken the thought aloud. She flushed at finding herself the center of attention. "I mean, Penny was after all of us in one way or another."

She glanced around the circle of friends, her heart warming at the sight of them. "But we came through it. There are some words that have been running through my mind lately that seem so appropriate." She hesitated, not sure whether she should go on.

Kate nudged her. "Tell us."

"It's a quote from Proverbs. 'If you search for good, you will find favor; but if you search for evil, it will find you.'"

Mason nodded slowly. "That's exactly it. Penny wanted something she didn't have, and she took the wrong way of getting it. I think, by the end, she'd lost all sense of what right is."

Jennifer smiled, secure in the acceptance of her friends and in Mason's love.

"Our reunion certainly turned out differently from what any of us expected, I guess. But I don't have any doubt that God brought good out of it for all of us."

Dear Reader,

Thank you for picking up this last installment of the *Reunion Revelations* series. All of the authors hope you've enjoyed our stories as much as we've enjoyed working together to write this series for you.

I always love writing books that include children, and little Alexis really touched my heart. I wanted so much to give her a happy ending, with parents who really love her. And it was a pleasure, too, to write about college friends who lost each other for years and then found each other again. I have some dear college friends who mean the world to me, even many years after our graduation, and this story was dedicated to them.

I hope you'll let me know how you felt about this story, and I'd love to send you a signed bookmark. You can write to me at Steeple Hill Books, 233 Broadway, Suite 1001, New York, NY 10279, e-mail me at marta@martaperry.com, or visit me on the Web at www.martaperrycom.

Blessings,

Marta Perry

QUESTIONS FOR DISCUSSION

1. Can you understand the conflict Jennifer faced when she longed to tell her friends about her past but was afraid to risk losing them? In the past, how have you struggled to balance two seemingly conflicting needs?

2. Mason has been driven all of his life by the lack of love his parents showed to him and their favoritism toward his brother. How do you think that makes him afraid to take on responsibility for someone else's happiness?

3. Jennifer's solid family background helps her deal with everything that comes her way, even though many might think she had a difficult time due to her mother's illness. Have you found that dealing with troubles can sometimes bring a family closer together? How?

4. Jennifer's dedication to children makes it impossible for her to refuse help to Mason and Alexis, even though it brought her close to heartbreak. What drove her, even when she was afraid?

5. Mason withdrew from God because he felt that God could never forgive him for his failures. The truth was that Mason couldn't accept forgiveness. What experiences have you had with God's forgive-

ness? Is there anything that you tend to hold back from God? What?

6. The scripture verse for this story is a very short one, but it packs some powerful meaning in a few words. Have you found this verse to be true in your life? How so?

7. Jennifer finds a community and acceptance in the friends she had made in college, even though she hadn't seen them for ten years. Reflect on your own friendships. Have some of them lasted for a long time, in spite of separation? Why do you think that is?

8. Mason eventually finds his way back to a relationship with God through the love and the responsibility he feels for his new-found daughter. Do you think we turn to God more readily when times are difficult? Why or why not?

9. Have you ever known anyone who blames everyone else for their troubles, as Penny does in this series? What are the results in that person's life?

10. How does a person search for the good? How have you searched for the good in your life, even when you've had problems?

11. What do you think it means that evil finds those who search for it? Do you believe a person can go so far that he or she can never find a way back to God?

12. Which is more difficult for you—to forgive some-
    one who's done wrong to you or to admit and
    accept forgiveness when you've done something
    wrong? Why?

13. I recently reunited with some college friends I
    hadn't seen in decades, and I was surprised at how
    little they had changed in personality and spirit. Do
    you suppose a person's attitude toward life is al-
    ready set by the time they're twenty or so? What
    could change it?

14. Do you think that Mason and Jennifer will have a
    happy marriage ahead of them? What changes and
    adjustments do you think they'll have to make?
    What changes have you had to make with your
    various relationships and friendships?

15. Do you feel that Alexis will find her own happiness
    after the difficult early life she's had? How will her
    relationship with God help her?

REQUEST YOUR FREE BOOKS!

2 FREE RIVETING INSPIRATIONAL NOVELS
PLUS 2 FREE MYSTERY GIFTS

YES! Please send me 2 FREE Love Inspired® Suspense novels and my 2 FREE mystery gifts (gifts are worth about $10). After receiving them, if I don't wish to receive any more books, I can return the shipping statement marked "cancel". If I don't cancel, I will receive 4 brand-new novels every month and be billed just $4.24 per book in the U.S. or $4.74 per book in Canada, plus 25¢ shipping and handling per book and applicable taxes, if any*. That's a savings of over 20% off the cover price! I understand that accepting the 2 free books and gifts places me under no obligation to buy anything. I can always return a shipment and cancel at any time. Even if I never buy another book, the two free books and gifts are mine to keep forever.

123 IDN ERXX 323 IDN ERXM

Name	(PLEASE PRINT)	
Address		Apt. #
City	State/Prov.	Zip/Postal Code

Signature (if under 18, a parent or guardian must sign)

Order online at www.LoveInspiredSuspense.com

Or mail to Steeple Hill Reader Service:

IN U.S.A.: P.O. Box 1867, Buffalo, NY 14240-1867
IN CANADA: P.O. Box 609, Fort Erie, Ontario L2A 5X3

Not valid to current subscribers of Love Inspired Suspense books.

Want to try two free books from another series?
Call 1-800-873-8635 or visit www.morefreebooks.com

* Terms and prices subject to change without notice. N.Y. residents add applicable sales tax. Canadian residents will be charged applicable provincial taxes and GST. This offer is limited to one order per household. All orders subject to approval. Credit or debit balances in a customer's account(s) may be offset by any other outstanding balance owed by or to the customer. Please allow 4 to 6 weeks for delivery. Offer available while quantities last.

Your Privacy: Steeple Hill Books is committed to protecting your privacy. Our Privacy Policy is available online at www.SteepleHill.com or upon request from the Reader Service. From time to time we make our lists of customers available to reputable third parties who may have a product or service of interest to you. If you would prefer we not share your name and address, please check here.

LISUS08

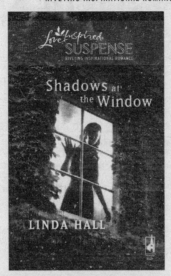

Love Inspired.
SUSPENSE

TITLES AVAILABLE NEXT MONTH

Don't miss these four stories in July

SHADOWS AT THE WINDOW by Linda Hall
Lily Johnson sings in the church choir and is engaged to
a youth minister...but not long ago, she was Lilith Java,
a singer in a rock band and witness to a drug deal gone
wrong. Lily tries to leave those memories behind, but
someone from her past isn't through with her yet.

TO TRUST A FRIEND by Lynn Bulock
Someone got away with murder, and forensic specialist
Kyra Elliott is determined to find the killer. Then a man from
Kyra's past, FBI investigator Josh Richards, is assigned to
the case, and Kyra has to let go of logic and act from the
heart.

DOUBLE JEOPARDY by Terri Reed
The McClains
When Anne Jones agrees to testify against a drug lord,
she's confident the Witness Security Program will protect
her...until her new identity is compromised. Soon, Anne's
handsome boss, Patrick McClain, becomes the only one she
trusts to keep her safe.

GRITS AND GLORY by Ron & Janet Benrey
Cozy Mystery
When a hurricane hits Glory, everyone runs for cover—
everyone except Ann Trask, the Storm Channel team, and
the dead man under the collapsed church steeple. Ann and
cameraman Sean Miller believe it was murder. Can they stay
safe with a killer on the loose?

LISCNM0608